CAN BATMAN SAVE THE CITY HE HAS SWORN TO PROTECT?

He didn't know how long he stood there, the wind whipping his cape around him, his thoughts heavy with doom. Batman had never admitted defeat before. Whatever the problem, he'd always believed that intelligence, integrity, and compassion could combine to overcome it. But how could he bring Gotham back from this? Maybe now was the time to admit he was beaten, that there were some wars even he couldn't win.

But, though his head told him the city was finished, his heart spoke a different language.

A bat-line snaked from his hand. Its grapnel caught some fifty feet away on the ledge of a building with great cracks running up its walls. One last glance over the city he loved . . . and then he was swinging away into the night—into the darkness and uncertainty of what had once been Gotham but was now No Man's Land.

BATMAN™
NO MAN'S LAND

ALAN GRANT

Batman created by Bob Kane

A
MINSTREL®
BOOK

Published by POCKET BOOKS
New York   London   Toronto   Sydney   Singapore   Gotham City

This book is a work of fiction. Names, characters, places and incidents are products of the author's imagination or are used fictitiously. Any resemblance to actual events or locales or persons, living or dead, is entirely coincidental.

A MINSTREL PAPERBACK *Original*

A Minstrel Book published by
POCKET BOOKS, a division of Simon & Schuster Inc.
1230 Avenue of the Americas, New York, NY 10020

Cover painting by Joe DeVito
Interior art by Stan Woch

ISBN: 0-671-03829-X

First Minstrel Books printing January 2000

10 9 8 7 6 5 4 3 2 1

A MINSTREL BOOK and colophon are registered trademarks of
Simon & Schuster Inc.

Printed in the U.S.A.

For my grandson, Elliot Michael Gray

Batman: No Man's Land was primarily adapted from the story serialized in the following comic books, originally published by DC Comics:

Batman: No Man's Land #1 (March 1999)
Batman #560–574 (December 1998–February 2000)
Detective Comics #727–741 (December 1998–February 2000)
Batman: Shadow of the Bat #80–94 (December 1998–February 2000)
Legends of the Dark Knight #116–126 (April 1999–February 2000)

With additional material adapted from or inspired by:

Batman Chronicles #16–18 (April, July, and October 1999)
Batman: Harley Quinn (September 1999)
Batman: No Man's Land #0 (October 1999)

These comic books were created by the following people:

		Writers:	Steven Barnes
Group Editors:	Dennis O'Neil		Bronwyn Carlton
	Mike Carlin		Paul Dini
			Chuck Dixon
Editors:	Jordan B. Gorfinkel		Ian Edgington
	Matt Idelson		Bob Gale
	Scott Peterson		Jordan B. Gorfinkel
	Darren Vincenzo		Alan Grant
			Devin K. Grayson
Associate Editor:	Joseph Illidge		Larry Hama
			Janet Harvey
			Lisa Klink
Assistant Editor:	Frank Berrios		Dennis O'Neil
			Kelley Puckett
			Greg Rucka

Pencillers:		Inkers:	
	Jim Aparo		Eduardo Barreto
	Jon Bogdanove		Sal Buscema
	Mat Broome		Robert Campanella
	Mark Buckingham		Randy Emberlin
	Rick Burchett		Wayne Faucher
	Sergio Cariello		John Floyd
	Guy Davis		Drew Geraci
	Mike Deodato		James A. Hodgkins
	D'Israeli		Andy Lanning
	Dale Eaglesham		Mark McKenna
	Yvel Guichet		Jaime Mendoza
	Paul Gulacy		Sean Parsons
	Dan Jurgens		James Pascoe
	Rafael Kayanan		David Roach
	Greg Land		Matt Ryan
	Alex Maleev		Bill Sienkiewicz
	Jason Minor		Batt and Aaron Sowd
	Tom Morgan		Phil Winslade
	Jason Pearson		
	Pablo Raimondi		
	Roger Robinson		
	William Rosado		
	Paul Ryan		
	Damion Scott		
	Frank Teran		
	Phil Winslade		

BATMAN

BRUCE WAYNE

ALFRED PENNYWORTH

ROBIN

NIGHTWING

THE HUNTRESS

COMMISSIONER JAMES GORDON

SARAH ESSEN

BATGIRL

ORACLE

CASSANDRA

DET. RENEE MONTOYA

THE JOKER

HARLEY QUINN

TWO-FACE

THE PENGUIN

MR. FREEZE

**SCARFACE &
VENTRILOQUIST**

**DET. MACKENZIE
"HARDBACK" BOCK**

POISON IVY

KILLER CROC

**DET. SERGEANT
HARVEY BULLOCK**

**CAPTAIN
WILLIAM PETTIT**

**NICHOLAS
SCRATCH**

PROLOGUE

What is a city without its people?

For the hundredth time, the thought spiraled through Batman's mind as he gazed at the darkened ruins that were once the mighty Gotham City. From his moonlit perch atop the dizzying heights of Wayne Tower, he had a panoramic view for miles around. And everywhere he looked, he saw destruction.

It had been two months since the earthquake struck, sending a shockwave that measured 7.6 on the Richter scale ripping through the heart of the bustling city. Streets cracked open like mud drying in the noonday sun. Buildings swayed, toppled, and collapsed as if they were made of cardboard. And people died—a hundred thousand was the official estimate, though no one would ever know the true toll.

Life in Gotham had always been hard, but since the quake it had become a nightmare. No power, no lights, no public services, no shops, no transportation. Criminals ran amok, secure in the knowledge there was little chance of being caught as the remnants of the police department were being run ragged. And with food scarce, even ordinary, decent citizens were willing to fight for a can of beans or a candy bar.

In partnership with Police Commissioner James Gordon, Batman had done everything he was capable of, and more. He'd rescued hundreds trapped in the rubble; led the expedition to save passengers on a crashed subway train fifty feet below the surface; even helped set up soup kitchens for the millions of earthquake victims. And all the while he was fighting crime.

But it wasn't enough. He was only one man. How could even he put an entire city back together again?

Now, he had come to the top of Wayne Tower, one of the few quake-proofed buildings that had withstood the catastrophe. Here he could see the steep price of his failure firsthand.

Batman swung his nightscope toward the waterfront and adjusted the focus, making a conscious effort to hold down the despair that welled up inside him.

A tide of humanity was streaming onto the bridges that led out over the water to the mainland. Refugees. Under the watchful eyes of the National Guard they swarmed away from Gotham like some massive column of ants. Most were on foot, their faces gray and ashen, hardly able to comprehend what was happening to them. They clutched whatever meager possessions they could carry in their arms: clothes, blankets, and their precious supplies of food. Since gas was at a premium, there were few cars.

The nightscope zeroed in on a family, shuffling in silent harmony onto the Trigate Bridge. Their shoulders were slumped in abject defeat, their movements jerky and mechanical as their minds fought to accept the fact that they were leaving their homes, their neighborhoods, everything they'd ever known . . . never to return.

As if afraid that the very gesture would bring on tears, not one of them looked back. Only the baby, held tight to her mother's chest, never took her eyes off the dark, receding city. She was crying, but only because she was hungry, not because her home lay in ruins. Not because Gotham was being abandoned like a sinking ship.

In an hour they'd all be gone. Only the criminals would remain, and those who refused to give up and leave the city that had housed them all their lives.

What is a city without its people?

Unbidden, the thought leapt again to Batman's mind. Although he fiercely opposed the evacuation, the decision hadn't been his to make—the politicians in Washington were responsible for that. They refused to declare Gotham a federal disaster area, so there was no government aid, no financial grants.

In his other identity, that of Bruce Wayne, Gotham's wealthiest citizen, he'd gone to the Senate to plead the case for his home. But he lost. Urged on by Nicholas Scratch—a religious leader with powerful political friends—the president himself had signed the order to close the city down completely. After the population was evacuated, no one would be allowed to enter or leave; the Army and the Air Force would see to that.

Why? Batman wondered. *Why does Scratch hate my city so much?*

Just then he felt a flutter of movement nearby, and flicked his gaze toward it. A bat flew past his cape, oblivious to his presence. Following its path for a moment, he watched as it swooped down over the broken buildings and rubble-strewn streets toward Gotham Cemetery.

Suddenly, in his mind's eye, Batman was an eight-year-old child again. He remembered that bleak and storm-tossed night all those years ago, when despair had first broken his heart. His parents had taken him to the movies to see *The Mark of Zorro*, his favorite film. It was on their way home that the madness began.

Shards of memory pierced him now as he recalled Crime Alley: a weasel-faced thug with cold, thin eyes and a gun in his hand . . . the rasping demand for money.

But Dr. Thomas Wayne, his father, was not a man who gave in to threats. There was a scuffle, the gun fired twice, and as running footsteps vanished into the night, young Bruce Wayne stood looking in horror at the bodies of his mother and father.

Two nights later, as lightning split the air and thunder rolled, a frightened Bruce knelt on the gravel by his parents' grave. But the fear in his heart was not of the elements, rather of the empty life he saw stretching away ahead of him.

"You haven't died for nothing, Mom . . . Dad," the boy whispered, his words lost in the swirling wind. Somehow, he had to make their deaths *mean* something.

A flash of lightning lit up the carved marble tombstone as he realized he would never see his beloved parents again. Cold rain mixed with the hot tears that flowed down his face.

"I'll avenge you!" he cried. "I don't know how, but one day I'll make Gotham a safe place!"

Yes, that was it: He would become the guardian of the innocent, the protector of the weak. He would dedicate his life to putting an end to crime.

Bruce Wayne had kept his promise, spending all of his adult life fulfilling it. When the sun went down, and the criminals claimed the streets, that was when the Batman took to the skies—the Dark Knight, an avenging angel whose only enemy was crime, and the evil men do to each other.

But could even Batman rescue Gotham City now?

The crowds on the bridge had thinned, until only stragglers were left, hurried on by the uniformed guards. Batman looked on in silence as heavy metal barriers were dragged across the entrance to the bridge and topped with razor wire. Then the soldiers retreated behind the crawling columns of refugees.

It was a full fifteen minutes before the sky suddenly lit up under the force of a massive, controlled explosion. The center of the bridge seemed to hang, suspended in air, for a long moment before it went plunging down into the waters of the Gotham River. As the smoke and dust cleared, tangled metal jutted from the crippled bridge, a hundred-yard gap between it and the other side.

Another blast, farther off, marked the end of the century-old Brown Bridge. A muffled roar and cloud of dust meant that the Novick Tunnel had been blocked.

Batman's eyes were expressionless slits in his cowl, but inside his emotions were in turmoil. This was his city, and he'd spent his life here. He knew its streets and alleys, its rooftops and its subways—knew it better than the men who'd planned and built it. He'd been its guardian while the city lived; he felt it was his duty to be there when it died.

He didn't know how long he stood there, the

wind whipping his cape around him, his thoughts heavy with doom. He'd never admitted defeat before. Whatever the problem, he'd always believed that intelligence, integrity, and compassion could combine to overcome it. But how could he bring Gotham back from this? Maybe now was the time to admit he was beaten, that there were some wars even he couldn't win.

But, though his head told him the city was finished, his heart spoke a different language.

A bat-line snaked from his hand. Its grapnel caught some fifty feet away on the ledge of a building with great cracks running up its walls. One last glance over the city he loved . . . and then he was swinging away into the night—into the darkness and uncertainty of what had once been Gotham but was now No Man's Land.

CHAPTER 1

THE SILENT CITY

From Oracle's Log: No Man's Land, Day 91.

The midnight air is crisp, the moon bright. From the window of my hideout, high in the Clock Tower, Gotham City stretches out around me like a ghost town.

Streets that once teemed with people are deserted and still. Not a single vehicle moves along them; there probably isn't a gallon of gasoline left in the entire city, and besides, most roads remain blocked with rubble from the earthquake. It feels strange, seeing a place that once was so alive, now abandoned and empty.

But it's the silence that affects me most profoundly. Once the night was full of noise—people laughing and talking, car horns blaring, snatches of music streaming from bars and radios. Now, the only sound to break the stillness is the occasional *pop* of a distant gun being fired, although it doesn't happen often. Like food and water, bullets are in short supply.

I used to hate the noise. Sometimes, when I wanted to think, I'd close the double-glazed windows to try and shut it all out. Now, I'd give anything to hear those sounds again. I never realized silence could be so depressing.

It's been three months since Black Monday, the day the Feds evacuated the population. Over the course of forty-eight hours, millions of refugees streamed out over the bridges and through the tunnels, before the National Guard destroyed them. The newly passed federal law made it illegal for anyone to stay behind; for the first time in my life, I broke the law. How could I go? I grew up here in Gotham. I love this city, warts and all.

And I wasn't the only one to stay in the ruins. My father, Police Commissioner James Gordon, didn't go; he and my stepmother, Sarah Essen, are still at their apartment less than forty blocks away. Along with the many cops who, through loyalty or just plain pigheadedness, remained with them, they're fighting hard to reestablish law in a place where law no longer exists.

But I haven't seen either of them in three months. They know I'm here, but they just can't reach me. Criminal gangs control the streets between us, and heaven help any outsider they find on their turf. Gang warfare erupted the moment the city was cut off. Through fear or force of arms, each gang laid claim to however much territory it was able to hold.

Other people stayed, too, thousands of old people, orphans, illegal immigrants, all the dispossessed who never had much of a life in Gotham anyway, and who wouldn't face anything better outside it. The gangs have become their new owners.

Worst of all was the news from Arkham Asylum—the home for the criminally insane. Two days before the bridges came down, Dr. Jeremiah Arkham threw open the doors and set his patients free. I can't blame him, really; he had no food for them, no power, no medication to keep the inmates under control. I know he had to make a terrible decision: keep these psychotic criminals locked up and watch them slowly starve to death, or release them, knowing they'd head straight back for the city that spawned them. Jeremiah is a good man at heart; in his place, I'd probably have done the same thing.

It didn't help Gotham any, though, to have maniacs like the Joker, Two-Face, and Poison Ivy descend on it all at once. Most of them had been gang leaders before they were caught and locked up in Arkham; now, like medieval warlords, they stake their claims to what they see as their turf, and fight with tooth and claw to keep it.

Two-Face has taken City Hall for his headquarters. Poison Ivy has camped out in Robinson Park. Penguin has set himself up as a sort of Fixer Supreme; from his base in the Iceberg Casino he trades and barters, swapping food and bullets for matches and batteries. Black Mask and his False Face gang have taken over the Fashion District, and the psychotic team of the Ventriloquist and Scarface has an iron grip on Newtown. There have been no definite sightings of the Joker, though rumor is he's cutting a swath of madness and death through Burnley and Otisburg in the northern sectors.

Joker . . . I wince at the very thought of him, and have to bite back my hatred.

I glance away from the window, down at my paralyzed legs, and a stab of regret shoots through me. I remember the way it used to be. . . .

No one, not even Dad, suspected that I, Barbara Gordon, was the avenger who called herself Batgirl. I remember the wind in my face as I swung through the canyons of Gotham's streets, and the song in my heart that told me I was alive and doing what I'd always wanted: fighting crime my own way.

Then came that terrible night when the Joker shot me in the back. The bullet lodged in my spine and my leg muscles just . . . died. No more would I take to the night air in my costume. My days of trading punches with the likes of Cat-woman and Killer Croc were over forever.

It took me a long time to overcome

the bitterness and resentment I felt, but finally I managed. If I couldn't be an action hero, I'd make myself into a hero of another kind. I became Oracle, the all-seeing eye. I established networks of informers to feed me news about the criminals. I acted as point person for Batman and his crime-fighting partners, Nightwing and Robin. Slowly but surely I rediscovered my happiness and self-esteem.

So when the Feds announced the city was to be evacuated, I knew I couldn't go. My computers run on solar-powered batteries, the only operational ones in the city. The data they contain is invaluable in fighting against the darkness that has settled upon us: maps of the city, the roads above and the sewers below; locations of secret underground food stashes and the old fallout shelters; files on every criminal who's ever broken a Gotham law.

Now I trade my knowledge with my informants, telling them where to find food as long as they promise to give me my share. Ironic, really—I'm still the all-seeing eye, only these days I don't see very far. Maybe I should change my name to the Chronicler. After all, someone has to record what's happening here . . . and no one's better placed to do it than I am.

If only I were still Batgirl! The city needs heroes now more than it ever did, but there are few around. I've heard that the Huntress, a ruthless vigilante, is still operating close by, but she's the only one. Batman ordered Robin to leave the day before Black Monday. Looking after the newly relocated, he's out in the suburbs, across the bay, only five or six miles away. But it might as well be a million.

Nightwing returned to his own territory, the port of Blüdhaven, also swollen with refugees. He's badly needed there.

As for Batman . . . I haven't heard from him for ninety-one long, bleak days and nights. No one knows where he is. There have been no sightings, no reports. For me, Batman and Gotham were always inseparable. When the city needed help, he was always there. But not now.

I can't believe he's abandoned us.

And if he hasn't . . . then where is he in our darkest hour?

The few thousand ordinary citizens that are left have almost forgotten Batman even existed. "If ever there was a Batman," they say, "he must have died in the quake."

I tuck my blanket more tightly around my useless legs, and look back out the window of the Clock Tower. The temperature has dropped, and moonlight gleams off the frost that covers the toppled buildings. Thick, dark clouds are rolling in from the north.

Soon, the first flakes of snow will start to fall. It's going to be a long, hard winter.

"Snow!" Zim Benson cursed. Impatiently, he brushed away the flakes that had fallen on the denim patch he wore on the breast of his jacket—the patch that proclaimed he was a member of the Street Demonz gang. "Snow's all we need!"

"No big deal, man." At Zim's side, his fellow gang member Genghis grinned in evil anticipation. He pointed toward the wooden slats nailed up over the windows of a derelict apartment building. They could just make out a dim light inside, flickering between the cracks in the window boards. "It's occupied. Means heat—and food!"

Zim hefted the nail-studded club he held in his right hand. "Then let's do it, and quick! I'm freezin'!"

The two Demonz moved swiftly across the road, their footsteps deadened by the thin carpet of snow. "Hit hard and fast" was their gang's motto—and the burly, shaven-headed Genghis lived up to those words as he shoulder-charged the thin slats that barred the doorway. They gave way with a loud crack; then he and Zim were inside.

"Madre de Dios!" a small, wiry man gasped in Spanish, and reached out for the iron bar leaning against the wall close to him. Zim's club swung in a wild arc and smashed into the man's shoulder. The man shrieked and fell back clutching the wound.

Genghis grinned as flickering candlelight illuminated the scene. The man, two women, and three children squatted in a circle on the floor, the three cans of beans they were about to share in the center. "Told ya, Zim—food!" Genghis's eyes lit up with anticipation. "And where there's a little, there's a lot. Right, granma?"

The old woman looked up at him through frightened eyes. *"Por favor, señor,"* she began, but Genghis cut her off sharply.

"Immigrants, huh? Illegals, I'll bet." He threw a glance round the dilapidated apartment. "So what else ya got stashed away here? Batteries? Clothes?"

"Hey, we can take the clothes they're wearin','" Zim suggested. He raised his club threateningly toward the terrified children. "Give us everythin' ya got—or th' kids get it!"

No one moved. Then Zim and Genghis whirled back toward the door as a hard, authoritative voice snapped from the doorway: "Gotham City Police! Drop your weapons!"

Commissioner James Gordon stood there in classic ready-to-fire pose, both hands holding his gun steady. Flanking him on each side were two other officers. Sergeant Harvey Bullock gripped a tire iron in his hand, while Renee Montoya spun a heavy length of chain in slow, menacing circles.

Zim and Genghis hadn't survived this long without knowing when they were beaten. The club and Genghis's knife clattered to the floor.

"Now," Gordon hissed quietly, "take off *your* clothes and get out of here."

"B-but it's snowin' outside," Genghis began to protest.

"It's what you were going to do to these poor folks," Gordon grimly broke in. "Tit for tat, that's the law now. So get naked, and get out. And tell your gang that this block is now in G.C.P.D. hands. Blue Boy turf. Anyone who breaks the law here will answer to us. Understand?"

Zim and Genghis nodded miserably as they stripped down to their shorts. Without another word they exited the broken doorway. Jim Gordon watched as they hurried off down the street, arms clasped across their chests in an effort to keep warm. Behind him, Montoya was talking to the family in Spanish, reassuring them they were now safe.

Under Gordon's command, the twenty or so police officers who'd stayed behind on Black Monday were expanding their territory.

Gordon stuck a hand in his overcoat pocket, and pulled out a spray can. Holding it a foot from the outside wall, he pressed his finger down on the release button. A thin jet of blue paint shot out, tracing "G.C.P.D." in large letters. Tagging, the gang boys called it. Marking their territory. Establishing turf. As if they were criminals, not cops.

He blanked the thought from his mind. These weren't normal times. The only law in Gotham was the law that he and his men brought. If this was how they had to do it, then so be it.

"Commissioner!" A thin young cop was coming toward him, wiping snow away from his thick glasses.

"What is it, Wilson?"

"Look what I've made!" Wilson held up a large flashlight. Taped across the glass was a cut-out stencil in the shape of a bat. "Watch, sir!"

Wilson flicked the ON switch, and a powerful beam of light leapt into the night. Where it struck the wall, thirty feet above their heads, it showed the distinct figure of a bat. "Just like the old Bat-Signal. If Batman *is* in the city, this'll get his attention!"

Wilson looked to his boss's face, expecting grateful approval. Instead, what he saw there stunned him into silence.

"No!" Gordon's hand shot out, striking the makeshift signal from Wilson's grip. The glass cracked as it fell to the sidewalk and the light went out. "There is no more Batman," he said between clenched teeth, his voice as icy as the street itself. "Batman gave up on Gotham, like everybody else.

He doesn't need us, so we don't need him! We're taking this city back—and we're doing it on our own!"

Turning on his heel, he stalked away.

"What was that all about?" Wilson asked, incredulous. "I thought the boss and Batman were friends?"

"They were," Harvey Bullock said gruffly. "But the Commish thinks the Bat-guy's deserted him. After all they've been through together, he feels betrayed. And I gotta say," Bullock finished passionately, "I don't blame him!"

Halfway across the desolate city, a three-time loser known only as Skunk crept through deep shadows toward a badly damaged building. Skunk had always been a parasite, stealing what he could, where he could, to make a living. It was harder in No Man's Land, but so what? There were still enough chumps left for him to prey on.

Earlier today he'd heard noises from inside the building. Now he meant to find out who had caused them, and what they were doing—and the foot-long bayonet he carried in one hand would convince whoever it was to cooperate.

The snow was thinning now as the wind drove the clouds out to the south. Suddenly the moon was visible again—and Skunk gasped as he saw what its light revealed.

Painted on the wall was a tag. This was someone's turf. But not just anyone's. The tag was sprayed in the stylized shape of a bat.

Gotta be a trick, Skunk thought. *There ain't no Batman no more!*

Despite the thought, he looked nervously up . . . and his heart almost stopped. Silhouetted against the moon was a dark figure, the jagged edges of its cape blowing in the wind like the wings of some supernatural beast.

Batman!

Skunk had never run so fast in his life.

CHAPTER 2

GANG WAR

Footsteps splashed in deep puddles as two teenage boys ran through the nighttime mist, their overcoats flapping against their legs. Fear lent speed to their desperate escape—they could hear their pursuers only fifty yards behind, gaining with every step.

The snow had lain for a week before it melted, leaving large pools of water everywhere. In many places, where the streets had been buckled or split open by the quake, the water had mingled with the rubble and debris, turning it to thick, clinging mud.

A few paces behind his friend, Donny Paxton sucked air deep into his aching lungs. He and Pete had been out on a scavenging expedition, looking for food to increase the meager supplies that had kept them alive. Both were orphans, inmates of the

Gotham Children's Institution; when the staff and other kids had fled on Black Monday, Donny and Pete were somehow left behind in the confusion.

They'd survived for more than three months, hiding out in the abandoned orphanage by day, skulking around the streets by night, looting shops for food. But now, it looked as if their run of good luck had come to an end. A half dozen members of the BadBlood street gang had appeared out of the darkness like ghosts, each of them holding an improvised weapon.

"Warm-lookin' coats, kids," the gang leader hissed. "You'd better give them to us. Call it a toll for using our streets!"

Donny and Pete didn't wait to hear more. Both knew that, even if they did as they were told and handed over their long, thick overcoats, it wouldn't end there. The gang would beat them up, or force them to reveal their hideout, and then raid it for whatever might be of use to them. Even as the gang leader's voice trailed away, they were both running.

"Stop them, ya dolts!" the leader snarled. A length of pipe whistled through the air, narrowly missing Donny's head before it clanged off a wall— and then the chase was on.

As they approached a broad mud pool, Pete leapt. A few paces behind, Donny saw his friend sail through the air and land safely on the other side. Heart pounding in his chest, Donny followed. But he'd mistimed it. His foot slid in the mud, and he crashed heavily to the street.

Pete stopped and looked back. No way Donny would be able to get up and run on before the gang reached him. Raising his arms in the air as a sign of surrender, Pete shouted to the gang: "Okay, we give up! You can have our coats!"

"Not enough, kid," the gang leader rasped. There was a twisted smile on his scar-pocked face as he reached out to jab the fallen Donny with the baseball bat he carried. "Runnin' away means ya gotta be punished!"

The club rose in the air and Donny cowered, trying to brace himself for the blow. But it never fell.

Instead, a sinister shape detached itself from the shadows nearby and hurtled through the gathering mist at the gang. There was a glimpse of a long, dark cape, its jagged edges whipping around the figure it hid. A black-gloved fist shot out from the darkness, and the gang leader fell like a stone.

Pete was stooping by Donny, trying to help him

up. Both boys froze, caught up by the spectacle unfolding in front of them. One of the gang lunged with a knife blade, but the caped figure ducked easily beneath the wicked swing. A boot swept upward in a perfect karate kick, taking the knife-man under the chin. He screamed briefly as his teeth bit into his tongue, then slid unconscious to the ground.

The newcomer didn't wait to see the effects of the blow, but kept moving, fists and feet a blur of speed. The boys had never witnessed anything like it; even the martial arts movies they'd watched at the orphanage seemed to be in slow motion compared to this lethal black shape. The other four hoodlums went down like tenpins.

"It-it's the Batman!" Pete stammered, incredulous.

Suddenly, the figure was looming over them. They could see the yellow bat-emblem on its chest, and the small points sticking up like ears from the mask that covered its face.

"No," Donny whispered. "It's a . . . woman! Please," he begged, as a black-clad arm stretched down toward him, "don't hurt us!"

"The Bat hurts only criminals." The figure spoke for the first time, grabbing Donny's arm and yanking the boy effortlessly to his feet. The voice was deep and full of controlled menace, but there was no disguising the fact—its owner was a woman.

The Batgirl turned away from the boys, pulling something from the pouched Utility Belt that circled her waist. There was a hiss of compressed air as she pointed the aerosol spray at the wall, and drew a large, golden bat-symbol on the bricks.

"This is my turf now," the voice grated. "I don't know where you kids have been staying, but there's a medical post a half dozen blocks from here. You'll be safe there."

A grapnel and line whirled in the figure's hand, then arced high to anchor itself on a stone gargoyle far above their heads.

"Tell your friends," the figure said, "as long as there are people in Gotham, there will be a Bat to protect them."

Then she was gone, vanishing back into the shadows of the night.

Donny and Pete stood gazing up, open-mouthed, for a whole minute. Their overcoats flapped around their ankles as they squelched off down the muddy street, and away from the fallen gang.

* * *

A mile to the south, Commissioner Gordon was hurrying to keep up with the long strides of his trusted detective, Mackenzie "Hardback" Bock. Though Bock stood well over six feet tall, his strength and muscles were only partially responsible for his nickname.

Bock slowed his pace as they approached the corner. From around it came the glow of a fire, the red light casting flickering shadows. At the foot of the broad steps that swept up to the marble façade of the Gotham Public Library, a group of men were huddled around a blaze, cooking some pigeons they'd caught.

There was a huge pile of books nearby, and whenever the flames died down a little, the men fed the fire another armful of volumes.

"Burning books to keep warm," Bock sighed. "That should be a punishable offense!"

That was the real source of his nickname, his love for books. While other cops spent their downtime doing crossword puzzles or reading magazines, Mackenzie Bock could seldom be found without a book in his hands.

Gordon shrugged. "Where would we lock them

up? We don't have a prison. And even if we did have, there isn't enough manpower for us to guard it."

Bock nodded resignedly.

Skirting the plaza, the two policemen moved on, their eyes continually darting around, looking for signs of trouble. They were on the street that marked the boundary between the territories claimed by two gangs—the Street Demonz and the LoBoys—and anyone caught here was considered fair game for either.

Staying in the shadows, they crossed silently over onto Street Demonz turf. Neither spoke a word as they crept on for another block, but Gordon knew they were both thinking the same thing. *If we're cops, how come we're acting like criminals?*

In the past week they'd liberated two more blocks and taken the people under their protection. But now Gordon had come up with a daring plan. Instead of risking his own men's lives in an attempt to wrest back Old Gotham, he proposed to play the gangs off against each other. That way, when they'd exhausted themselves fighting, Gordon's Blue Boys could move in and mop them up.

Some of his men hadn't been too happy with this proposal. All their working lives they'd been crime fighters. Now their own boss was proposing that they actually *instigate* crime.

"We're not a police force anymore," Gordon had argued. "We're an army. It's our job to reclaim this city, no matter how we have to go about it!"

"I'm with the Commissioner!" Pettit, the ex–S.W.A.T. team leader, exclaimed. "We go in there, kill a half dozen Demonz, then stand back as the fireworks erupt!"

"We don't *kill* anyone," Gordon said curtly. "I said we're an army—not an army of murderers!"

We're a law unto ourselves, he thought—and suddenly he remembered Batman. The vigilante had always been a law unto himself. Now, Gordon could see what might have made him that way. Perhaps Batman had had everything taken away from him, too—just as the city had been taken away from Gordon. Maybe they were the same after all.

Angrily, Gordon brushed the thought away.

"Old Gotham? Downtown . . . that's where the Clock Tower stands, isn't it?" Officer Foley had asked.

Gordon's steely gaze held Foley's as the Commissioner snapped: "What's your point?"

"Isn't that where your daughter lives, sir?

Couldn't that be interpreted as some kind of ulterior motive?"

"You can interpret it any way you like," Gordon said, a chill in his voice. "I'm going to start a gang war. Are you with me or not?"

They were—and now he and Bock made up the advance patrol. Each carried an aerosol can, and at the corner of every block they paused to spray the LoBoys' tag on top of the Demonz' own cartoon-style devil. The Demonz would think their rivals were intruding on their turf, launch some sort of retaliatory attack—and Gordon's men would step in when the violence was over.

"That should do it," Gordon said finally. They'd sprayed dozens of LoBoys symbols on walls and doorways, even on the bodywork of an overturned car that was slowly rusting on the street. "Let's go!"

"Well, well! What have we got here?"

Gordon's heart sank as a sneering voice spoke behind them. Three Street Demonz stood there, their homemade slingshots loaded for action. Nestled in the sling of each was a one-inch steel ball bearing.

"Looks like we're gonna have to teach the LoBoys a lesson." Another Demonz smiled, ready to fire his deadly missile. Imperceptibly, Gordon's hand moved toward the pocket of his trench coat where he kept his pistol.

Suddenly there were three loud bangs in quick succession and two of the Demonz collapsed soundlessly to the ground. The third stood for a moment, as if stunned, staring down at the blood that spurted from the bullet hole in his chest. He groaned, then fell on top of his buddies.

"Pettit!" Bock said in amazement, as the ex–S.W.A.T. captain stepped forward out of the shadows. A thin wisp of smoke curled from the barrel of the gun in his hand. "You followed us!"

"I did good, right?" Pettit replied smugly.

"You—you killed them!" Gordon accused, gesturing toward the slumped hoodlums. "There was no need to do that!"

"Excuse me, sir." Sarcasm dripped from Pettit's voice. "But I thought you might be grateful, seeing as how I've just saved your life. After all, you're the one who said we're not cops anymore. We have to play with the villains at their own game!"

Gordon glared at the officer, but didn't reply. How could he, when everything Pettit said was true? The Commissioner's thoughts were bleak as the three trudged back through the streets toward East-lyn.

"And there's a bonus," Pettit said brightly. "When the Demonz find their homies dead, they're *really* gonna be ticked with the LoBoys!"

From Oracle's Log: No Man's Land, Day 99.

The war between the LoBoys and the Demonz has been raging for two days. Estimated fatalities so far: forty-two gang members, with an unknown number wounded. Every now and then I see a plume of smoke, as one side or the other torches a building in their opponents' territory.

So far, the civilians have managed to keep out of the firing line. Who knows how long that will last?

But I can't focus enough to worry about it. I've been getting reports for a week that tags in the shape of a bat have been appearing all over the Liebek District. I didn't believe my informants at first. If Batman *was* back in town, why hadn't he contacted me? And why hadn't there been sightings of him?

Yesterday, I found out why. One of my contacts at the medical center called me on the battery phone. Said he'd over-heard two kids talking; seems they'd been attacked by a gang, but were res-cued. By someone in a bat-costume. A woman!

I felt sick when I heard. *I'm* Bat-girl. Even if I can't wear the costume anymore, that role belongs to me. Who gave someone else the right to play the part? Batman? How dare he!

Who is she, I wonder?

Questions, questions . . . and I don't have any answers.

CHAPTER 3

REUNION

"Can you swim, old man?"

The thug called Dooley twisted the man's arm farther up his back, forcing his face down toward the dark waters of Gotham River, a hundred feet below. Dooley's three companions laughed.

They were all standing on the very brink of what had once been the Trigate Bridge. The four-lane highway came to a sudden, jagged stop, with the muddy waters swirling far beneath. Only a mile away, the stump of the mainland end of the bridge stood like a mirror image. It was all that remained since Black Monday.

"I said, can you swim?" Dooley snapped, and the old man spoke for the first time.

"Not in there," he replied, his voice half-muffled by his thick beard. ". . . Mines."

"Clever," one of the other thugs sneered. "That's right—they say the Feds mined the river in case anyone tried to escape. But we don't know for sure."

"And our boss, the Penguin, wants us to find out," Dooley added. "That's where we can help each other. See"—Dooley's grin widened—"we're gonna push you in. If you explode, we'll know it's mined. If you don't . . . why, you can just swim to the mainland and escape!"

The thugs laughed again as Dooley grabbed the man's beard. "Time to go now," Dooley said—then broke off in astonishment as the beard came away in his hand. "What the—? It's a fake!"

"But I'm not!" The low, gravelly voice came from above. Before they even had time to look up, its owner was among them in a swirl of black cape and flashing fists. He moved faster than any human being had a right to, and his every blow unerringly found its target.

In mere seconds, Dooley and his men were lying unconscious on the broken roadway, and the newcomer was turning anxiously to the gang's victim.

"Are you all right, Alfred?" he asked.

The man nodded, pulling off the low-brimmed hat and false mustache that completed his disguise, revealing his true identity: Alfred Pennyworth, Bruce Wayne's loyal butler and Batman's faithful friend. When he spoke, his voice now had a rich English accent. "Rather like the old days, don't you think? An innocent in danger, and then the Batman arrives, just in the nick of time!"

"Sorry about that," Batman said ruefully. "In most ways, it's *not* like the old days. All the rubble and collapsed buildings—they slowed me down getting here."

"Not to worry," Alfred said cheerfully. "At least our little information-gathering exercise was a success. Firstly, we know my homing transmitter works, or you wouldn't have arrived at all! Second, we know that these, er"—he gestured toward the fallen thugs—"*gentlemen* are working for that unsavory villain, the Penguin."

There was an angry roar as Dooley regained consciousness. He lunged suddenly to his feet and charged, a large lump of concrete clutched in his hand.

Dooley swung, but Batman easily stepped aside. Carried off balance by his own momentum, Dooley stumbled against the end of the bridge, banging his head and dislodging some loose masonry. The stones plunged downward, and an instant later there was a loud explosion as they hit the water.

"There's the answer to your question," Alfred muttered. "The river *is* mined!"

Batman nodded curtly at the dazed Dooley. "Go back and tell the Penguin that. And give him a message from me: His time will come!"

Together, Batman and Alfred turned away, heading back into the city. It had been three months since Batman had seen action, three long months in which he and Alfred had plotted, planned, and schemed for the war they knew was coming. Now, they were ready to start to fight back.

Finally, Batman's crusade was about to begin. It had been the hardest three months of his life, sitting on the sidelines while his beloved city deteriorated. But Batman knew it was the best choice—the only choice—in the place called No Man's Land.

Jim Gordon allowed the war between the Demonz and the LoBoys to go on for another day before he decided it was time to interfere.

His men surged through the old city streets,

wielding clubs and tire irons and even the boomerangs that someone had found in a looted sports store. Each carried a gun, but no one wanted to use it. Who knew when they'd ever be able to replenish their small stash of ammuntion?

Weak and disorganized from their intergang feud, the Demonz and the LoBoys put up only token resistance. Within an hour, police officers had secured every block in a twenty-street radius, including their own police headquarters.

A real morale booster! The thought gave Gordon a lot of pleasure. Of course, the gangs would have long since looted the place, emptied it of everything they could carry out. But still, it was a psychological victory.

The few hundred ordinary citizens left in the area had come out onto the streets as soon as they'd realized what was happening. Both gangs had been brutal overlords, and now the people wanted their revenge. They joined with the police, using pots and pans and bricks, anything they could lay their hands on, as weapons.

Soon, the captive gang members were penned in a circle of angry humanity.

"Hold them till I get back!" Gordon ordered, as he hurried over toward the Clock Tower.

From her window high in the building, Oracle had seen everything. She released the automatic bolts on the steel shutters that had kept the Tower secure from gang attack, and seconds later heard footsteps hurrying up the stairs.

She was throwing open her apartment door as he arrived. "Dad!"

"Barbara! It's so good to see you!" Jim Gordon flung himself on his knees beside the wheelchair and wrapped his daughter in a crushing hug. With no mail and no phones, it seemed like years since they'd been in contact.

They had a lot of catching up to do.

It was half an hour before Gordon went back down to the street, only to find his men arguing about what to do with the captive gang members.

"We can't hold them," Foley was saying. "We can't spare men to guard them, and we don't have supplies to feed them!"

"What if we let them stay?" Renee Montoya suggested. "They could work for us."

"They're criminals through and through," Pettit told her with ill-disguised disdain. "First time we turn our backs, they'll knife us and reclaim their turf! I say we shoot 'em all, as an example to every other gang in Gotham!"

"There'll be no more murder while I'm in charge," Gordon barked. "We send them on their way. Under penalty of execution if they return."

"And you'll be prepared to enforce that, sir?" Pettit asked.

Gordon didn't flinch. "Yes." But he knew that the day he willingly committed murder was the day he would give up. Forever.

Oracle received the call that evening.

"I thought you'd like to know," the gravelly voice at the other end of the line said, "I'm back."

Her heart soared. *Batman!* In reality, she knew that no one person could make much of a difference to the hell that Gotham City had become. But just knowing he was there sent a rush of adrenaline coursing through her.

"So it was you," she said, "tagging all these buildings? Spray-painting the bat-symbol all over the place?"

There was a pause, then: "Not me," Batman murmured.

"And who is this new Batgirl?" Oracle demanded. But the line had already gone dead.

* * *

Downtown at night had always been a dangerous place. Since Black Monday, it had become ten times worse. It was too large for any single gang to lay claim to, though they had all looted its shops at some point. It was the No Man's Land of No Man's Land, where a hundred criminals lurked but none ruled the roost.

The thick mist that lay over the area disguised the movements of the dark figure that crept over the rooftops. Downtown stood on a bed of sandstone, soft rock that had been badly damaged by the earthquake. Buildings tilted at crazy angles, while others had collapsed completely.

It was almost an hour before Batman found what he was looking for. Perched still as a statue on a sloping roof, he used his infrared lenses to pierce the mist and make out what was happening on the street below.

A one-sided fight was in progress.

Roach Daimler was a big guy; he'd spent years learning martial arts in his teens, knowing that his criminal career might one day depend on them. But he was nowhere near a match for the slim, black-masked girl who was in the process of giving him a serious beating.

"Enough!" Daimler panted at last. Once again he tried to pick himself off the ground, but his arms just didn't have the strength. "I give up! Wh-what do you want of me?"

The wearer of the Batgirl costume stared down at him contemptuously. "I want you to move out of Downtown," she spat. "Go to any gang boss you like—just make sure you never come back here!"

"You got it, sister!" Daimler hauled himself upright, wiping blood from his mouth with the back of one hand. His eyes flicked toward the travel satchel that lay on the sidewalk close by. "Just let me take my things—"

"No!" Batgirl swept up the satchel in her hand, and unzipped it. Inside were dozens of pill bottles, all stamped GOTHAM CHEMISTS. "That's why you're leaving," Batgirl hissed. "Because you've been sell-ing stolen drugs to the gangs. Well, no more!"

She upended the bag suddenly, and Daimler cursed as the bottles tumbled out, falling between the wide bars of a sewer grille. He clenched a fist. "Why, you—" he began angrily, but Batgirl paid no heed.

"If you're still in my sight in two minutes' time," she said softly, in a tone that told Daimler she meant it, "I'll show you some of my advanced moves."

Still cursing under his breath, Daimler took to his heels. Batgirl watched as the mist swallowed him up. He was someone else's problem now.

"Nice costume."

The comment startled her, but even as she whirled to face the newcomer she automatically adopted a defensive crouch.

"You!" Under the mask, her mouth dropped in surprise. Batman stood there, looming like a phantom as wisps of mist swirled around him. Quickly, she recovered her composure. "I didn't think you'd approve," she shrugged, gesturing toward her costume.

"I don't," Batman said curtly.

"You haven't been around," she tried to justify herself. "I thought . . . I thought that the city needed a Bat. Especially now." She paused for a second, but he didn't reply. "If you're really back, you're going to need help."

"No," Batman told her. "Gotham's too dangerous. That's why I sent my other partners away. I know what has to be done—and I'm not looking for any help."

Batgirl shrugged again. "I've been doing it for weeks now. And I intend to keep on doing it, whether I have your approval or not."

Batman was silent, his mind sifting through all the possibilities. He was going to have enough problems on his hands fighting criminals; the last thing he needed was a war with someone who was on the same side as he.

"I don't approve," he said finally. "But if you continue doing what you've been doing, just one thing—" His finger pointed to the golden bat-emblem she wore on her chest. "Don't disgrace my symbol."

As Batman moved quickly away and disappeared into the murky night, the woman in the Batgirl costume permitted herself a small smile. Batman didn't approve—but he wouldn't stop her. It wasn't quite the same as having his blessing . . . but it was a good start.

And he hadn't even tried to figure out who she was!

Swinging away through the rooftops, Batman's mind was racing. The woman had disguised her voice, hoping he wouldn't recognize her. But to a trained detective like Batman, even a person's body language was enough. He knew precisely who "Batgirl" was: Helena Bertinelli, the vigilante also known as the Huntress.

Helena's father had been a Gotham mob boss. When rival gangsters attacked him at home, Helena had been the only survivor. Ashamed of her father's crimes, and determined to stop the gang wars that regularly erupted in the city, she had adopted a black leather costume and become a vigilante.

Huntress and Batman had often argued, because her tactics were vicious and extreme. Unlike him, she didn't hesitate to use deadly force against her criminal enemies. But Batman had always known her heart was in the right place; she cared for Gotham City just as deeply as he did. It must have cost her a lot to give up her own identity in order to become Batgirl, but she'd done it for the sake of the city. He respected that.

Just as he respected her decision now.

CHAPTER 4

WHO'S THE DUMMY?

"Who did this?"

Jim Gordon turned up his overcoat collar and stuffed his hands deep into his pockets in an effort to shut out the chill morning wind that blew in from the river. Emotions seethed through him as he gazed at the bright, golden bat-symbol sprayed on the wall.

Bock shook his head. "We don't know, sir. I sent Watson and Ramirez on a reconnaissance patrol. This"—he gestured at the painted tag—"is what they reported."

"Sir?" Renee Montoya's voice was hesitant. She knew only too well how her boss felt about Batman now, but she had to ask anyway. "Do you think it means . . . he's *back*?"

"No!" Gordon said harshly. "It does not mean

he's back! But what it probably does mean is that there's some prankster at work!"

"But, sir, how can you be so sure?"

Gordon turned away, shoulders hunched up against the biting wind. "Where he's concerned," the Commissioner grated, only half under his breath, "you can never be sure of anything!" He was aware of the bitterness and resentment in his words, but he made no effort to conceal it. "Batman let us down," he went on. "If he ever did come back, it wouldn't be like this—spraying paint on a wall. That was never his style."

"So what do we do, sir?"

Gordon thought for a moment. "It might give people the wrong idea," he decided. "They might think that this street is safe. Best thing we can do is paint over it!"

"Who did dis?"

The words seemed to come from the ugly wooden dummy manipulated by the small, chubby gang boss called the Ventriloquist. Together with a half dozen members of his gang, he stood staring at the bat-tag that had appeared overnight on a wall deep inside their territory.

"Now, Scarface, you shouldn't let it annoy you," the Ventriloquist said appeasingly, looking nervously at the dummy, as if he was afraid of it.

The psychiatrists at Arkham Asylum said the Ventriloquist was insane; a "split personality," they diagnosed. He himself was a mild-mannered, unprepossessing man—but his true, evil nature was manifested via Scarface, the dummy he carried with him everywhere. At least, that's what the experts said. Ventriloquist had a different take on things. The dummy had been carved out of the wood of the old gallows tree in Blackgate Island Prison, and Ventriloquist was convinced Scarface had a supernatural life of its own.

"Annoy me?" Scarface snapped. "Of course it annoys me, ya no-good grainless geek! What if it means da Gatman is gack?"

They say that the letter "B" is the hardest of all for anyone to get right when they're throwing their voice, that it comes out sounding like "G." It was something the Ventriloquist had never mastered. Often, his gang had to think hard before they realized just what Scarface was supposed to be saying.

"He wouldn't dare show his face here!" Ventriloquist's lieutenant, a giant of a man who'd been nicknamed Rhino ever since he was in school, shook his head in disbelief. "He wouldn't stand a chance against us!"

"I know dat," Scarface said. "An' you know dat. Gut does da stinkin' Gatman know dat?"

The dummy's head lowered for a moment, as if it was thinking. When it jerked upright on the end of Ventriloquist's arm, its glass eyes glittered malevolently, as if it truly was alive and not just a block of carved wood dressed like the mobster Al "Scarface" Capone.

"Awright—here's what we're gonna do. We're gonna send da Gatman a message." The dummy's arm shot into the air, waving its little machine gun over its head. "Gring me some innocent sap an' I'll shoot him dead! Dat'll show Gatman we ain't to ge trifled with!"

"Are you sure about this, Scarface?" Ventriloquist asked. "I mean, that would be murder."

"Shuddup!" the dummy roared. "I'm da goss of dis gang! I say what goes an' what don't!"

Rhino threw a glance toward the group of people who'd gathered to watch. They were mostly the underclass of Gotham society, those who hadn't left the city because they had nowhere else to go. Only they hadn't realized they'd end up being bossed around by a small, fat lunatic and his gun-toting puppet.

"You heard the boss," Rhino said loudly. "Anybody want to volunteer, or do we just pick a victim at random?"

There was silence from the group. They had plenty of complaints about their lives—but not surprisingly, none of them was willing to voluntarily die. Fear ran through them as each one prayed that Scarface would choose somebody else—anybody except them.

A disheveled man stepped forward. He was taller and broader than most of the others, but his face held that same defeated look they all wore.

"So . . . ya wanna die?" Scarface asked, swiveling the tiny tommy gun.

The man shook his head. "No . . . uh, no, sir," he faltered. "I was hoping maybe you and I could do a deal. I have something you might be interested in." He dug his hand inside his jacket, and when it came out it held four bullets.

"Gullets?" Scarface demanded. "Where did ya get dem?"

"Found 'em," the man admitted. "A big box.

There must be a thousand bullets in it. You can have them all, if only you don't kill me!"

"Take us to dis gox."

"If I do that," the man said, "what's to stop you from just shooting me anyway? From my point of view, it'd be safer if I could meet you tonight—alone."

The dummy's eyes seemed to take on a cunning look. "Yer a shrewd guy," he said pleasantly. "Awright. Chivers Street, nine o'clock. Don't ge late, or it'll go worse for you!" Scarface turned to Rhino. "Get dese creeps to work. I wanna see 'em diggin' for loot. Da Murray Guilding is as good a place as any to start."

With Rhino in the lead, the men headed off down the street. Scarface waited till they were out of earshot before he began to laugh.

"What's so funny?" the Ventriloquist wanted to know.

"Da gullet-guy," Scarface leered. "We need more ammo, so I'm playin' along with him. Gut once da ammo is in our hands—" His finger tightened round the trigger of his mini-gun. "Goom! Da guy gets shot anyway! Dat way we get da gullets—plus we still get Gatman's attention!"

His hollow laughter echoed down the street.

* * *

"Are you sure this is wise, sir?" Alfred asked.

It was late afternoon and darkness was already falling, but in a secret hideout beneath Wayne Tower, a pair of hurricane lamps cast a pallid glow.

"I mean, acting like a common criminal by spraying tags is bad enough," the old butler went on, "but arranging to meet Scarface alone . . . well, if you'll pardon my saying so, it's crazy! *He's* crazy! Surely you realize it will be a trap?"

"I know," Bruce Wayne nodded. His hand reached to the top of his head, and he slowly peeled off the latex face mask that had allowed him to infiltrate Scarface's territory. "But the Ventriloquist doesn't know *I'm* setting a trap for *him!* Is the box ready?"

"It will be soon, sir," Alfred assured Bruce, as he screwed a small block of metal with attached wires into the wooden box lid. "However, I should point out that Scarface is likely to have at least a dozen gunmen with him. Don't you think you should call in some aid? I mean, Master Robin or Master Nightwing would be only too delighted—"

"No," Bruce said brusquely. "I have to do this myself. Gotham is my responsibility. I made an oath to protect it."

Bruce glanced around the inside of the hide-out. Its walls were lined with shelves groaning under the weight of books and manuals. Boxes of tools and canned food were stacked in one corner, while a specially designed Batcycle leaned against a pillar.

"It's taken us three months to set up this network of Batcaves," Bruce continued, "but now they're ready, and it's time I fought back against the evil that's contaminated Gotham. The myth of Batman has been neglected. It's up to me to breathe fresh life into it!"

Alfred sighed. He knew better than to argue with his employer when Bruce was in this kind of mood. The old butler made a final adjustment to the box he had constructed, and stood back. "It's all yours, sir."

Bruce pulled on the cape and cowl that would transform him into his other identity as Batman, Gotham's Dark Knight. He sighed, then said softly: "Don't worry about me, Alfred. I have to do this my own way."

A thin drizzle was falling as the Ventriloquist, carrying his foul-mouthed dummy, Scarface, stumbled through the darkness and approached the Chivers Street rendezvous.

The gang boss wasn't alone. At least a dozen of his men were hidden close to the meeting place.

"He's not here," Ventriloquist said, disappointed.

"Naw," the dummy snapped, "but da gox is!" His ugly wooden head twisted to call out into the night: "Awright, guys, ya can come out now."

His men gathered expectantly around the large wooden crate that stood just outside the cracked and damaged entrance to the subway station.

"A thousand gullets!" Scarface leered. "Dis'll give us da firepower we need to take over half da city!"

Together they all leaned forward in anticipation as Rhino used a tire iron to pry the box's lid off. The dummy's glass eyes reflected the light from one of the hoodlums' flashlights; they seemed to glitter greedily. He started to laugh as Rhino gripped the lid and ripped the last few nails away—

Abruptly, a blinding flash exploded from inside the crate.

"My eyes!" Rhino cried. "I can't see!"

Several of the thugs coughed uncontrollably as thick gas poured from the empty crate.

"Tear gas!" someone shouted. "It's a trap!"

Batman swooped down from the rooftop where he'd watched the scene play itself out. Alfred's booby trap had worked perfectly. Now it was time for him to play his part.

Half-blinded by the brilliant flash, choking and retching from the tear gas, Scarface's gang put up little resistance as Batman hurled himself into their midst. He used a high karate kick to catch one man on the jaw, then swept on to strike a second. Before they hit the ground, Batman was taking the fight to their companions. The only one to offer real resistance was Rhino, but even he soon crumpled under Batman's fierce onslaught.

It was over in two minutes. Scarface lay silent on the roadway, next to his unconscious owner and his thugs. Batman looked at the fallen gang and felt a small glow of satisfaction. If the rest of his battles were as easy as this, it wouldn't be long before Gotham was back under his control.

Nightfall, and the silence was so profound you could almost hear it.

Jim Gordon walked swiftly out of the area controlled by his Blue Boys, waiting until he was well clear before switching on his flashlight. He didn't want any of his men—or his wife, Sarah—to know where he was going, or what he intended to do.

Or whom he was meeting . . .

He'd walked these streets a thousand times before at night, but always when the street lamps were on. Now, the entire city was without electricity, and it seemed to him like a different world as he hastened toward City Hall.

Again and again, he asked himself if he was doing the right thing. Again and again, the answer came—no. But what choice did he have? In keeping with his intention to reclaim the whole city from the criminals who controlled it, the next target for his Blue Boys was the territory centered on the Iceberg Lounge and Casino. Penguin's headquarters.

Gordon's men wouldn't stand a chance against Penguin's fifty armed thugs. The police needed help, and there was only one source of aid he could turn to: another gang boss. So when the message had come to him from Two-Face offering a deal, Gordon knew he couldn't just ignore it.

He stopped two blocks away from City Hall. Peering around a corner, he could see armed goons standing guard at a half dozen strategic locations.

"Commissioner! You came."

Startled, Gordon pointed his light toward a shadow-filled doorway, and saw Two-Face grinning back at him, the smile only on one half of his grotesquely disfigured face. Once, Two-Face had been on the side of law and order; he was District Attorney Harvey Dent, who used his keen mind and deep understanding of criminals to wage his own war against them.

However, all that had changed the day Boss Maroni turned on him in court. Dent had just finished a hard-hitting speech, calling for the gang leader to be jailed for his crimes. Enraged, Maroni had thrown a vial of powerful acid straight into Dent's face, leaving the D.A. hideously scarred all down his left side.

The worst effect had been on Dent's mind. From being a paragon of virtue and upholder of the law, he had turned almost overnight into an insane, embittered criminal. Every decision he made was decided by a toss of his silver dollar. If the unscarred side landed face up, he did good; if the scarred side came up, then he chose evil.

It was the unscarred side that had suggested he meet with Jim Gordon.

"I'll come straight to the point," Two-Face said bluntly. "You need help, and I can give it. With my men attacking his western flank, Penguin won't stand a chance against your frontal assault. Only question is, What do I get from you in return?"

Gordon sighed. He hated doing a deal with a murderer like Two-Face, but his experience in the war between the LoBoys and the Demonz had taught him that playing thugs off against each other was a ploy that would work well.

"I'll return the favor," Gordon said quietly, fighting back the shame he felt. "You'll need help one day, and I'll be there."

Two-Face nodded, and reached out his hand. "Deal," he smiled. "Shake on it."

Gordon wanted nothing more than to pull his gun and place the madman under arrest. But he knew Two-Face didn't take chances; somewhere, out of view, a marksman had Gordon in his sights.

"Deal," the Commissioner said at last. But the note in his voice was not one of triumph. It was disgust.

CHAPTER 5

BATTLE BRIEFS

The rain hadn't yet reached Amusement Mile in the city's northern sectors.

A gaunt figure sat in a deck chair in the middle of the dark roadway, ignoring the sounds of gunfire that came from nearby, gazing up at the stars that twinkled brightly in the night sky. He'd never seen the stars like this before—the lights of Gotham had always obscured them.

He ran his fingers through his bright green hair and thought how beautiful the stars were.

How would it feel if I ruled the entire universe? he wondered.

There was a final gunshot, and as the echoes died away the figure sat up and watched the group that approached him. A flashlight swung in his direction, reflecting off the pure white skin of his face.

"We got 'em, Joker," a voice called out.

The Joker grinned widely, stretched, and leaned back in his deck chair. He smiled through impossibly red lips as he surveyed the motley group of captured gang members who stood before him, their hands held high in the air. Behind them, five of the Joker's own gang held guns at their backs. "Looks like you boys should have surrendered when I gave you the chance."

"P-please, Joker," one of the captives stammered. "Don't hurt us! We could join your gang. We could help you!"

"I'd like that!" Joker leapt from the chair in one fluid motion, not stopping till he stood directly in front of the pleading gangster. "But there's a problem," he went on, his face jutting out, his insane eyes staring deep into those of the terrified man. "Everybody in my gang has to know how to laugh. Like this—" He broke off, and started to laugh in a crazy, high-pitched voice. "Hee hee hee! Haw haw! Hyuk hyuk!"

The gangster looked at the Joker in terror. He knew that he and his buddies should never have tried to stand up to the Clown Prince of Crime. But maybe, just maybe, there was still a way out. The man opened his mouth, swallowed once, then started to laugh. "Hee hee hee! Haw haw!"

The other captives stared for a moment, then they too fought down their fear and started to bray and hoot. Within seconds, all twelve of them were making more noise than a zoo full of hyenas.

Joker watched them, smiling happily. He did so like to hear the sound of men laughing. Abruptly, he turned away from them and motioned to his lieutenant, Harley Quinn. Resplendent in her harlequin costume, she was almost as crazy as Joker himself.

"Now, Harley," Joker said softly. "Kill them. While they're happy."

Then he settled back down in his chair, eyes riveted on the heavens above. Once the northern sectors were completely his, he'd march on the rest of Gotham. And then . . . well, who knew?

There was a big universe out there. He'd like to hear it laughing, too.

Before he destroyed it.

"I'm doing this for Gotham!" Jim Gordon reminded himself for the hundredth time.

He and his Blue Boys had spent the past hour infiltrating the Penguin's territory, sneaking through tumbledown buildings, adopting positions where their boomerangs and bows and arrows would be able to do their awful work. Now they were ready, surrounding the Iceberg Lounge and Casino, waiting for the sign that Two-Face was attacking the other flank.

Gordon was racked with guilt over his deal with the evil Two-Face. Sure, he'd be expanding the Blue Boys' turf, and a successful operation tonight would mean the city would be that much safer. However, the battle would also strengthen Two-Face; Gordon knew the ex-D.A.'s gang would head straight for Penguin's personal hideout, and steal all the weapons, ammunition, and food that the Penguin had stashed away.

"I have no choice," Gordon muttered to himself. "It's the only way. Somehow I have to restore civilization to Gotham. If that means siding with criminals, then it's the price I have to pay!"

A sharp burst of gunfire split the night, coming from several blocks away. It was Two-Face's signal. "All right!" Gordon yelled to his men, as Penguin's gang came spilling out of what had once been Gotham's glitziest casino. "Attack!"

Twenty cops moved forward. Despite his guilt, despite his shame, Jim Gordon was at their head.

From her window high in the Clock Tower, Oracle scanned the streets below with her infrared night-sights. As she peered through them, the whole world seemed to have turned green—except for the bright human shapes that she knew meant trouble was coming.

The gang boss known as Black Mask had long since thrown away the mask that for years had hidden his disfigured face. Gotham itself was disfigured, he reasoned; he no longer needed to hide his secret identity. What did it matter if he was recognized now?

Unknown to Jim Gordon, Two-Face had also made a deal with Black Mask. While the Blue Boys were attacking Penguin's lair, Black Mask and his False Face gang were going to pull a double-cross and invade the cops' turf. With the cops busy elsewhere, it would be easy.

Oracle's heart sank as she watched them heading directly for the Clock Tower. Black Mask's men were a lot more determined than the Street Demonz had ever been. Once they seized the

Tower, they'd have a perfect base to launch their invasion. And there was nothing Oracle could do about it, except . . .

She swiveled her wheelchair, and reached to snatch up the sniper's rifle that her dad had insisted she always keep by her. Even touching the gun made her feel queasy. She'd never shot at anyone in her life before, but maybe if she brought down Black Mask himself, his gang might scatter in disarray.

Leaning on the windowsill, Oracle raised the rifle and sighted carefully down the long barrel until it was centered precisely on Black Mask's chest. Her finger tightened on the trigger, then relaxed again.

No! The word screamed in her mind. *I can't do this—I can't shoot a man in cold blood, even a criminal!*

Gritting her teeth, Oracle pulled herself together. She had no choice. She *had* to shoot him or she'd lose everything—her hideout, her supplies, her invaluable computer records. Maybe even her own life. What use would she be to Gotham then?

Sighing deeply, she raised the rifle sights back to her eyes. What she saw made her gasp.

A dark figure was swinging down from a rooftop,

the scalloped edges of its cape streaming out from behind. *Batman!* she thought.

The hero let go of the bat-line and dropped toward the gang, both feet lashing out simultaneously to knock down two False Facers. Black Mask realized at once what was happening and started to bark out an order. He broke off abruptly as a Batarang spun through the air, and its weighted edge struck him between the eyes. He fell to the street, senseless. Then the attacker was among the gang, hands a blur, tossing pellets of knockout gas that burst at their feet, quickly enveloping them in choking fumes that sent the men slumping unconscious.

Oracle almost cheered out loud. Until she realized that it wasn't batman at all. Sure, the newcomer wore a batlike costume and fought just like her friend. But through the magnification of the powerful rifle sights, she saw that it wasn't even a man. It was the new Batgirl!

Oracle turned away from the window. How ironic that the old Batgirl should be saved by the new one. Although she knew she should feel happy, her heart was like a stone in her chest, and the tear that slid down her cheek was one of bitter regret.

*   *   *

It was six months almost to the day since the earthquake had struck Gotham.

In the first few seconds, as the ground rippled and buildings shook and fell, the roof of the YWCA building on Drew Avenue had collapsed. It crashed down through the upper floors, destroying the dormitories where dozens of girls slept, turning the rooms into unmarked tombs. Only one girl had escaped the carnage: a seventeen-year-old girl of Asian descent, who'd found the presence of mind to hide beneath the sturdy beams of the stairwell as plummeting masonry and screams filled the air around her.

Mute since birth, the girl hadn't left the building for months. She existed on the stocks of canned food heaped in the basement pantry, drinking rainwater that she collected in Styrofoam cups. Many times since, she'd looked out the windows at the desolate city; she'd seen the gangsters on the streets, heard the gunfire in the deep of night. And she'd made the decision to stay exactly where she was, until the day things got better.

But tonight, the teenager wasn't alone in the shattered building.

Mr. Zsasz was one of Gotham's most twisted villains, and one of Batman's most dangerous foes. To Zsasz's deranged mind, the world of man was hell. He believed that by killing people, he was sparing them the pain of life and sending them to a better place. Of course, none of his victims would ever have agreed with that—but Zsasz had never asked them.

For long months now he'd been moving stealthily through the ruins, looking for survivors. Each time he'd found a solitary citizen, cowering in fear and darkness, Zsasz had done his terrible work.

Creeping along the debris-strewn first floor of the YWCA, Zsasz saw the telltale signs of occupancy: discarded food cans, carefully positioned cups half full of water. He felt a warm glow spread through him; tonight he would help another unfortunate soul leave this grief-stricken world.

Without warning, the girl leapt at him out of the darkness. A swinging karate kick connected with Zsasz's hand to send the knife blade spinning away.

Zsasz was a well-muscled, powerful man, standing a full foot taller than the girl who attacked him. But she moved with blinding speed, raining blows on him from all kinds of impossible angles. Finally, a straight-arm chop dug deep into his belly. Zsasz gasped and doubled over, as the girl's fist slammed like a rocket into his jaw.

Did he have a gang? she wondered. *Will there be more like him?*

She had no intention of waiting to find out. Gathering together her few possessions, stuffing as much food as she could carry in a knapsack, she slipped out of the building and onto the silent road outside.

That's where Batman found her.

From Oracle's Log: No Man's Land, Day 110.

Batman came to see me tonight. I had so many questions to ask him about the new Batgirl, but when I tried, he just said, "Later."

He wasn't alone. There was a girl with him, a pretty teenager with raven-black hair. Seems she took out Mr. Zsasz all on her own. Impressive. But she can't speak. I've taken to calling her Cassandra, for no other reason than I like the name. Batman asked me to look after her, and to try to find out more about her. It'll give me something to do during the long hours when no new information comes in.

Batman told me he'd taken Zsasz to Blackgate Prison, which had suffered little damage in the quake. The warden and his guards all left on Black Monday, abandoning their prisoners. Dad had wanted to start using Blackgate again but didn't have sufficient manpower. Batman managed to get around that problem; he's made a deal with some of the toughest inmates. He's appointed them wardens, with orders to keep the others in line or face his wrath. In return, he's providing them with food.

Penguin escaped from Dad, though, slipping away during the confusion of the fight. Bad news, I know——but Dad seems to be taking it especially hard. I tried to talk with him about it, but he just mumbled something about Two-Face being a double-crossing snake, and cut me off brusquely.

Heroes in cahoots with villains. I never thought I'd live to see the day!

Batman still hasn't paid a visit to my dad. I guess maybe their friendship really is over.

CHAPTER 6

THE LOWEST EBB

"Sometimes I wonder why we're doing this."

Batgirl's voice reflected the weariness she felt in every muscle of her body. In the past few weeks she had helped Batman run a major blitz on minor criminals: They'd arrested the TallyMan, a trigger-happy gunshark who hires out his services to the highest bidder, and nipped the plans of Maxie Zeus in the bud. Zeus believes he is the reincarnation of the king of the Greek gods and is convinced he will one day rule over a restored Gotham City. Now, he's making his plans from a secure cell in Blackgate Prison.

"I mean," Batgirl went on, "how can we ever win? And even if we do, what do we have to show for it—a shattered city, and a few thousand destitute citizens?"

She and Batman were hurrying through the darkness of the old subway tunnel that led from the Batcave under Sixth Avenue to the one on the fringes of the City Hall district.

"The city can be rebuilt," Batman replied. "But it's a living thing. And people are its lifeblood. If that lifeblood becomes contaminated by evil, the city might never rise again."

They squeezed through the narrow gap that led into the chamber Batman had turned into a Batcave, one of a dozen he'd made throughout the city during the three months when he'd been "missing." He'd known full well that organized crime would clamp its grip on Gotham as soon as the bridges and tunnels were blown; to stand any chance of restoring order, Batman had to be able to fight from a position of strength.

As his flashlight beam played over the stacks of food and tools he'd stockpiled, he finished what he'd been saying: "Only we can defeat that evil."

Batgirl reached out to take a bottle of high-energy drink from a crate, wondering about the incredible resilience Batman seemed to possess. She was pleased that, in recent days, he had come to trust her more. "So," she said lightly, trying to shrug off the exhaustion that dogged her, "what evil do we go up against next?"

"I'm going to take down Two-Face," he told her. "There are certain files I need to retrieve from the vaults in the Hall of Records."

"Why?"

"Just a hunch that we might need them some-day. But the only way in there is to defeat Two-Face first."

"That's a tall order," Batgirl mused. "Perhaps we—"

"This is one job I'm doing alone," Batman said in a tone that brooked no argument. "I want you to stay here and guard our territory—the dozen or so blocks we control. Any one of the gangs would be willing to invade if they knew the turf was unguarded."

Batgirl wanted nothing more than to lie down and sleep for twelve hours. But she steeled herself; if Batman could hold out, then so could she. "I won't let you down," she said with quiet confidence.

"Are you sure we're doing the right thing, Jim?"

Sarah Essen's voice was no more than a whisper. She and her husband were crouched beyond a jagged heap of debris piled up at the side of a road. There was no moon tonight, and visibility was almost nonexistent. Though she and Jim couldn't see them, she knew that twenty of the Blue Boys were staked out in their own hiding places, waiting for Gordon to give the signal that would launch their attack.

"I'm not sure of anything anymore, Sarah." He chewed thoughtfully on his lower lip. "I only know that Killer Croc and his mob are holed up less than a hundred yards away—and that if we don't stop them, they'll go on killing and looting till there's nothing left."

Sarah hesitated for a moment. Killer Croc was a mutant, born with a strange skin disease that made him look more reptile than man—and gave him almost superhuman strength. What he lacked in intelligence, he made up for in sheer brute savagery, and a dozen of Gotham's most violent criminals had flocked to join him. "Croc is the most dangerous foe we've faced so far," Sarah began. "Wouldn't it make sense to try to contact Batman?"

"No!" Her husband's voice didn't rise above a whisper, but there was no disguising its harshness. "I thought I'd made it perfectly clear—we don't need him! We can take back Gotham without his help."

"Look, we've both heard the same rumors. We *know* Batman's in the city," Sarah persisted. "You've been trying hard to deny that fact, but you can't ignore him forever. What will you do when your paths finally meet?"

"I'll cross that bridge when I come to it," Gordon snapped. "Who knows? I may even arrest him!" He turned away from her abruptly, checking the clip of bullets in his pistol. "All right," he hissed into the darkness, "get ready to move! Now!"

Then he was on his feet, pistol cocked in one hand, flashlight blazing in the other. All around them, the night was split with the beams of a dozen flashes as the Blue Boys followed suit. Together they started to run toward the half-destroyed hotel where Croc had set up his temporary headquarters.

Well, I had to try! Sarah thought with resignation. She'd hoped that Jim's anger with Batman would fade once he realized the Dark Knight hadn't run out on him.

Instead, it seemed to be growing even stronger.

"This court is now in session!"

Two-Face banged the small wooden gavel down hard on the tabletop and stared at the four frightened thugs who stood before him. They were in the council chambers, deep inside City Hall. Once, civic leaders had argued and debated here; now it served as Two-Face's kangaroo courtroom. Half a dozen hurricane lamps were positioned around the chamber, their steady glow illuminating the beads of sweat that stood out on the faces of the accused. From the perimeter of the room, several of Two-Face's men watched the proceedings, one with his gun trained on the prisoners, just in case.

"You are charged with belonging to an illegal gang, namely, Penguin's," Two-Face went on. "How do you plead: guilty, or not guilty?"

None of the men answered; each was afraid that if he was the first to speak, Two-Face would use him as an example to the others.

"You!" Two-Face pointed at the tallest and strongest of the hoodlums. "Speak. Explain yourself."

The man glanced up, watching the gang boss's silver coin flash in the light as he tossed it in the air and caught it again in the same hand.

"S-sure," the man stammered, "we were in Penguin's gang. But we didn't have a choice. He needed muscle, and we needed the food he was willing to pay. As soon as the cops drove him out of the Iceberg Casino, we figured we were fighting for the wrong guy. That's why we came to you."

The mass of scars that covered the left half of the ex-D.A.'s face were livid in the lamplight, and his disfigured eye gleamed coldly. "I find you all guilty as charged," he declared to the men. His silver coin was poised on the edge of his forefinger, ready to be flicked into the air again. "The coin shall decide your punishment. If the scarred side lands facing upward, you're all dead!" His thumb flicked the coin high, and every eye in the chamber followed it as it spun through the air.

Suddenly the door burst open, and one of Two-Face's lieutenants rushed in, his face red with effort, his breathing hard and labored. "We're under attack, boss!" he gasped. "Three men down, out on the east perimeter. We think it's Batman!"

Two-Face froze. *Batman!* The spinning coin fell to the desk with a metallic clang; landing on its edge, it spun there for a moment before toppling over on its side.

"This court is adjourned," Two-Face said quickly, "until you bring me the Bat-vermin's head!" He gestured to the four prisoners. "Issue them a weapon each," he commanded. "They're fighting on our side now! Go!"

Two-Face waited till everyone emptied out of the chamber, then glanced down at his coin. The scarred side lay face up—the symbol for death. Two-Face grinned evilly to himself, then sat back in his chair to wait.

What was that noise?

Batgirl jerked herself out of the light sleep she'd sunk into. Stationed high on a ledge that ran along the top of an undamaged building, back pressed against the rough concrete wall, she was finally overcome with exhaustion. Despite every effort, her eyelids had grown heavy and her thoughts faded away as she found refuge in much-needed rest.

But down on the street, something was happening.

Peering down through the nightscope Batman had given her, she stifled a gasp of shock. There were at least thirty hoodlums moving along the road below, strung out in twos and threes, armed with knives and tire irons and other improvised weapons.

Bringing up the rear, surrounded by six men with pistols, was the Penguin.

Batgirl froze for a moment. Her every instinct told her to take the fight to the enemy, to swing down among them and neutralize as many as she could. But she was tired, and her body ached from the exertions of the past few days. Besides, the criminals were so far apart, her gas pellets would be ineffective. Surely even Batman himself wouldn't try to engage a criminal army of this size.

Her mind numb, her thoughts leaden, Batgirl rose to her feet and stumbled off across the rooftops.

"Aaagh!"

The scream cut through the night air, and Jim Gordon's heart lurched. He recognized that voice—it was Foley!

The Commissioner swept the beam of his flashlight through the fallen timbers of the four-star hotel, his eyes scanning the wide ballroom for signs of movement. At the far end, a massive figure stood erect, as if immune to the bullets that crisscrossed the entire area. Killer Croc! His scaly hide glistened in the light as his powerful muscles hoisted Foley above his head, then threw him to the ground. The officer's scream broke off as he lapsed into unconsciousness.

A barrage of shots rang out, and Jim cursed as one struck his flashlight. The impact made him drop it, the lamp shattering on the ballroom floor as he dived for cover.

Other Blue Boys flipped their lights off as more shots chattered out of the darkness. There was a yell of pain, close to his side, and Jim knew that another of his men had taken a bullet.

Killer Croc might be an unreasoning monster, but he knew the tactics of war. Although Gordon's men had knocked out every sentry they could find, they never suspected that some of Croc's fighters had stationed themselves on the balconies of the hotel's first floor. The policemen had marched straight into an ambush.

Gordon knew he had no choice. "Fall back!" he yelled at the top of his voice. "Retreat!"

He backed away toward the hotel foyer, Sarah close to his side. Just then a figure rushed at them out of the darkness, and there was a sharp boom as Sarah fired at almost point-blank range. The gangster went down in a crumpled heap.

More shots followed, and Jim and Sarah dived behind the splintered wood of the reception desk. As bullets thudded around them, they bobbed out and in again, firing back, trying to cover their men as they retreated toward the main entrance.

Hardback Bock was the last one out, half-carrying, half-dragging a wounded cop. Sarah and Jim unleashed one last volley, then sprinted for the exit and the darkened streets that spelled safety.

Twenty-one policemen had followed Jim Gordon inside. Only sixteen made it out.

The air was filled with the flash of guns and the whine of bullets.

Running along the first-floor corridor of City Hall, Batman dived behind an ornately carved pillar a mere instant before a salvo of slugs thudded into it. The flare of the guns let him know exactly where the sentries were positioned, and without looking he reached out and hurled a handful of smoke pellets.

He heard them shatter against the wall, then the sounds of two men, their curses quickly turning to coughs and gasps. Already moving, infrared lenses in place, Batman sprinted past them through the thick, billowing smoke.

Hurricane lamps spread their glow in dozens of places, piercing the gloom; Batman knew this marked him out as a moving target for any gunman who got him in his sights. Ahead, he could see the wide spiral staircase that ran down to the ground floor. Batman's plan had been to descend without being noticed, and from there gain entry to the basement vaults where all the city records were held.

But four of Two-Face's men were spread out on the stairway, ready to mow him down as soon as he was in range. Batman's eyes flashed with anger, not at his foes, but at himself. He'd vastly underestimated the sheer numbers in Two-Face's gang.

A barrage of shots splintered the floor around his running feet; it looked as if he was going to pay a serious price for his error.

Suddenly, Batman altered course, zigzagging across the wide hallway to a huge leaded window that had somehow survived the earthquake and its aftershocks. Pulling his cape up over his head with his left hand to protect his face and eyes, with his right hand he whipped a bat-line and grapnel from his belt.

The window shattered in an explosion of glass as Batman went through it headfirst. The grapnel shot from his hand, anchoring itself on a high cornice.

By the time the thugs reached the window, he was gone.

* * *

"I failed you."

Batgirl's mask hid the guilt on her face, but not her shame-filled eyes.

"You're not the only one who failed tonight." Batman's voice was low and grim. "I underestimated Two-Face. They drove me out."

That only made Batgirl feel worse. She could imagine the shock and pain Batman must have suffered when he retreated to his own territory only to find it, and the people to whom he'd given refuge, taken by the Penguin. Everything he'd worked for all these weeks, gone in a single night. And she had been too exhausted even to put up a fight.

He'd found her, lost in misery, on the roof of a building half a mile away.

"You trusted me, but I fell asleep on the job like some amateur bungler!" Slowly, Batgirl reached up to grasp the top of her mask. She paused, as if reconsidering, then tore it off with deliberate finality.

By the faint light of the stars, Batman saw Helena Bertinelli's face.

"I'm sorry," she said, and dropped the mask to the roof. "I'm not used to being responsible to someone else. I don't like it. Especially when I fail. It means I betrayed your trust."

"What are you going to do?" Batman asked.

Helena shrugged. "Batgirl is no more," she said sadly. "I'll continue this war in the guise I know best—the one where I answer only to myself. I'm going back to being Huntress."

"You know what they say, sir." Alfred tried hard to make his voice sound reassuring. "We learn by our failures."

Batman had returned to the Batcave under Sixth Avenue, his shoulders slumped in abject defeat. In a low voice, he related the night's happenings to his aging retainer. The news that Alfred had for him from Oracle was equally dispiriting: Gordon had lost five men and been routed by Killer Croc.

"We fought against evil," Batman said heavily. "And we lost." Wearily, he lowered his head into his hands, his whole body posture reflecting something Alfred had rarely before seen in his master: defeat. As if all the fight had gone out of him.

"This is a serious setback, yes," Alfred admitted, "but we have to believe we can still win the war!"

"I can't do it on my own." Batman's voice sounded as exhausted as Batgirl's had, just an hour earlier. "It's too much. Even for me."

"Then that is the lesson you have learned, sir," Alfred said, almost triumphantly. "No one man can do what must be done to save Gotham City. But perhaps, with the right help . . . ?" He let his voice trail away suggestively.

Batman sat motionless, considering Alfred's words. He remembered the months of preparation, readying the Batcaves and setting up supply lines. Everything was still in place; all he really needed was the aid of people he could trust.

"Yes!" Batman said softly, and Alfred heaved a sigh of relief as he saw that the light of defiance once more gleamed in Batman's eyes. "With the right help, we can still do it!" His hand reached out to snap on the power to his radio transmitter. "I'll call Oracle. She'll know where to find them!"

"Indeed she will, sir." Alfred smiled broadly. He knew how hard it was for anyone to accept that he was wrong—even the Batman. It takes a true hero to admit to having limitations.

It takes an even greater hero to make amends.

CHAPTER 7

RECONCILIATIONS

From Oracle's Log: No Man's Land, Day 163.

Winter ended badly for all of us. Thank heaven it's the first day of spring. Cue warm sunshine, with plants and weeds growing out of broken buildings and cracks in the street. Amazing how quickly life can spread when it has the chance. I guess we have to be like that—put down roots, hold firm, and refuse to budge for anything.

There are hardly any pigeons left in the city; their nests were raided for eggs. Lots of rats, though, living on garbage and rotting food and human waste. With the first rays of sunshine, the lack of sanitation became an immediately identifiable problem. Gotham really stinks!

As always, it's getting harder to find food. But spring brings renewed hope. . . .

"It's been nearly six months since we were in the city. How do you feel about returning?"

Nightwing pulled back hard on the joystick, and the lightweight glider banked steeply into a turn. Beside him, Robin was staring out the window. Far below, the lights of Gotham County curved in a bright arc around the waters of the bay. But on the other side, across the bridges that no longer existed, Gotham City itself was a black, shapeless mass.

"It's like the heart of darkness," Robin said quietly. "A war zone. And to be honest, it feels really weird coming back!"

Neither of the young heroes had seen Batman, or even communicated with him, since he'd exiled them on Black Monday. It had been hard for both of them; neither wanted anything more than to help their mentor restore the shattered city. Instead, he'd declared it was too dangerous, and sent them away. Now, it seemed he'd changed his mind.

Suddenly, a thin beam of intense light lanced up

from the center of the darkness below. As it touched a cloud, it cast a wavering image of the Bat-Signal, shining in the Gotham sky for the first time since Black Monday.

"There's our marker," Nightwing announced briskly. He punched the button that transferred responsibility for the glider to the automatic pilot; then he and Robin checked that their parachutes were in order.

"Ready?" Nightwing smiled.

Robin nodded tersely. "Let's do it!"

Seconds later they were plunging down through the night air, following the Bat-Signal to its source. Their parachutes snapped loudly as they billowed out; lost in thought they dropped toward the silent city below.

Batman stood immobile on the roof of the Clock Tower, his face expressionless as he watched the twin 'chutes descend. Although he'd only meant it for the best, he knew that Nightwing and Robin deeply resented his decision to exile them. How would they feel now that he'd recalled them?

The two young men touched down simultaneously, as Batman switched off the Bat-Signal; the

less it was seen, the better. Who knew what criminals it might attract, buoyed with the knowledge
that almost the entire city belonged to them?

The trio stood in silence for a long, awkward
moment, none of them knowing what to say. Then
Robin darted a glance to the side, out over the city.

"Wow, but it's dark here!" he said, and his irre-
pressible grin broke the tension.

"That's why I've asked you to return," Batman
said simply. "I want to put the lights back on. But I
can't do it alone. I need your help."

Nightwing and Robin stared at him in surprise.
Silhouetted against the stars, he looked calm and
unshakable, the solid rock they had always depended
on and trusted. They were used to his giving orders,
planning his strategy with grim intensity, saying precisely what he wanted them to do. He'd never asked
for their help before—and though they could only
guess at the circumstances that had led to it, both of
them knew what an effort it must have cost him.

"You don't need to ask twice, boss," Nightwing
said. He tried to keep his voice low and steady, but
somehow he couldn't stop it from cracking with
emotion. "You need us, we're here. That's the way
it'll always be."

Batman gave an inward sigh of relief. "I'm glad to hear it," he told them sincerely. "But before we start planning, I want you to meet the newest member of the team—"

He gestured toward the deeper shadows in the center of the roof, and a figure stepped forward. Her face was completely covered by a black mask, and a dark, jagged-edged cape wrapped her body. On her chest, in bright gold, a bat-emblem shone.

Robin's jaw dropped in astonishment, and Nightwing could only stare as Batman finished: "—Batgirl!"

From Oracle's Log: No Man's Land, Day 165.

I worked for long days and weeks with the girl Batman brought me. She could communicate only in grunts and gestures, but she has a quick mind and learns fast. Her story, when she was finally able to make me understand it using sign language and drawings, was almost beyond belief.

She doesn't seem to have a name, and is happy with the one I have given her: Cassandra. She was born in Korea; her American mother died in childbirth, and the man who raised her, Cain, brought her up alone. Unfortunately, he was one of the world's top assassins and was determined the girl would follow in his footsteps.

Convinced that speech was unnecessary for a hired killer, Cain never taught the girl how to talk. Instead, he spent endless hours demonstrating different styles of martial arts to her. She was a natural learner, and by the age of seven or eight she'd mastered several fighting disciplines. By the time she was ten, Cain decided her skills were ready to be tested.

Having stolen her childhood, he now wanted her to commit murder.

Cain sent her to infiltrate the palace of one of his many enemies. There she'd sneaked into the man's bedroom at night and stood over him, her fingers held rigid, ready for a death-strike.

The next thing she remembered was blood on her hands, and her mind screaming in horror at the evil she had done. She knew then that she could never do it again—but she also knew Cain would try to make her.

Confused and frightened, she turned

tail and fled into the night. Too afraid to go home and face Cain, she headed for the mountains. She lived there for seven years, eating berries and whatever animals she could catch with the weapons she fashioned for herself, all the while never seeing another human being.

Poor child! So innocent, yet she's suffered so much. My heart goes out to her. It's incredible, not only that she managed to survive in such a hostile environment, but that she hasn't gone insane with the effort.

When she learned that Cain's men were still searching for her, she knew it was time to leave. Traveling by night, she made her way to one of the country's many seaports and stowed away on the first vessel she came to. It was bringing cargo to Gotham City.

The boat docked one day before the earthquake . . . and the rest, as they say, is history.

I told Batman everything I learned about her. He tested her skills and abilities, and before I realized what was happening, the world had a new Batgirl.

I didn't know how to feel at first.

I'd been so upset when the first new Batgirl appeared, stealing my costume and—or so it seemed to me—my very identity. When Batman told me she was really Huntress, my blood boiled. But then she quit, and in a mean, selfish way I felt pleased that she hadn't justified Batman's trust in her.

Now he's trained Cassandra specifically to fill my old role. Strangely enough, I think I'm coming to accept it.

In fact, I feel proud of her.

"We have to work this out, Jim."

Jim Gordon froze at the sound of the voice, the plastic watering can in his hand halfway to the plant-pots. It was many months since he'd heard it, but Batman's deep, gravelly voice hadn't changed at all.

"There's nothing to work out," Gordon stated, not even looking around at the black-garbed figure who he knew stood behind him.

It was evening, and the setting sun had turned the sky bloodred. Gordon was in the small garden at the back of his Eastlyn apartment, tending to the rows of seeds he'd planted. It was strange—he'd never been a gardener; he and Sarah had always hired a man to come in and do what had to be done to keep their small patch green and flowering. However, since Black Monday, Gordon had been doing the work himself. It helped to fill in the long hours of life without any of civilization's benefits. It gave him time to think, to reflect. And in a strange way, it made him feel even closer to Gotham, as if working the soil, turning a wasteland of weeds into something ordered and beautiful, was a small-scale version of what he wanted for the entire city.

Slowly, deliberately, he finished watering the rows of swaying seedlings before he straightened up. "Are you still here?" he asked coldly, seeing Batman standing still as a statue, silhouetted by the sun.

"Look, Jim," Batman said steadily, holding the other man's piercing gaze, "I'm here to say I made a mistake. I went about things in the wrong way—"

"I'll say you did!" It was as if Batman's words had unleashed the barriers that held back the anger in the policeman's mind. "Ten years we worked together. Ten years with me inside the law, and you outside it! Ten *years* of helping each other in every way we could, because we both fought for the same thing. Justice."

Gordon broke off, then repeated the word, bitterly this time: "Justice? There isn't any justice in this world! The federal authorities abandoned this city. Okay, I could take that. Most of the people went, too. I accepted that. It was their right. Just as it was my right to stay and try to put the whole mess back together again. But *you . . .*" His voice took on an ugly, sneering quality. "You deserted me when I needed you most!"

Suddenly, Gordon's anger was spent, to be replaced by a deep, heartaching weariness. "Ten years of friendship," he sighed, "and you didn't even think enough of me to fill me in on your plan, much less say good-bye."

For the first time, Batman found himself seeing his actions from Gordon's point of view. It made him sad to know his friend thought he'd betrayed him. "It wasn't like that, Jim," he said quietly. "I had to disappear. I had to get ready for the war I knew was coming. So I spent three months in preparation, storing up food and fuel for when I—when *we*—would need it most. My mistake was in thinking I could do it alone. I know now that I can't. I need help."

"Do you remember the old days?" Gordon asked suddenly, as if he hadn't heard Batman's words. "It used to be so simple. We were the good guys, and we went out and caught the bad guys.

These days, it's hard to tell the difference. Decent folks will kill for a crust of bread or a pigeon's egg. They need order so badly, they'll accept the leadership of any gang boss who can give their empty lives a sense of meaning."

"Yes, I remember the old days." Batman's eyes were far away as memories flooded through him. He and Gordon had saved each other's life dozens of times. "I'm here to ask if we can't go back to the way we were then."

"How can we?" Jim cried impassionedly. "Whatever your reasons, I feel you betrayed me. How can I ever trust you again?"

Batman was silent, deep in thought. Then he reached one of the hardest decisions he'd ever made. His hand grasped the loose material at the back of his cowl. "Perhaps I should show you how much *I* trust *you*," he said simply, then tugged on the cowl.

Batman's secret identity of Bruce Wayne was known to only a handful of people—among them Nightwing, Robin, and Alfred. Should his identity ever be revealed, his crime-fighting days would be finished. Over the years he'd gone to great lengths to preserve that secret, even from Jim Gordon.

"No!" As soon as he guessed Batman's intention,

Gordon whirled away from the costumed hero. "Stop! I don't want to know!"

He knew exactly what Batman's gesture meant: It was an act of reconciliation, of making up this stupid feud which somehow seemed to have sprouted and grown without any effort. But it was a gesture Gordon didn't need.

His back still to Batman, he said steadily, "It isn't the man behind the mask who matters to me. What matters is that you, whoever you are, show me the respect that I've earned from you!"

"You have it, Jim."

The cowl was back in place as Jim Gordon finally turned, his right hand extended. Batman raised his own hand, and they shook. The way friends do after an argument.

"One more difference between now and the old days," Batman remarked. "We were loners then, both fighting crime in our own way. Now, we don't have any option: For better or worse, if we want to restore civilization to this city of ours, we have to play as a team."

By the time their plans were made, the sun had long since set.

CHAPTER 8

SCRATCH!

Mr. Freeze's ice palace towered a hundred meters into the air, like a giant's hand clutching at heaven. Millions of tons of ice had been molded and sculpted into fantastic battlements and towers that glittered and sparkled under the spring moon.

Freeze had been one of the inmates turned loose by Jeremiah Arkham on Black Monday. Unable to live at normal temperatures, he was forced to permanently wear a cryogenic suit that kept his body at zero degrees.

A tall, powerful man, Freeze headed straight for the city; only in Gotham would he find what he needed. Once there, he had no difficulty forcing a group of stay-behind bums to help him dig deep beneath a collapsed building.

It had taken them almost a week, but finally Freeze's secret lair was exposed. Savoring his anticipation, he'd pulled out four large, flawless diamonds from the vault that held them, and inserted them in the terminals on his chestplate. Immediately he was flooded with cryogenic power.

"I'm back!" he cried out in triumph. A jet of freezing air sprayed from the tubes in his glove, freezing his unwilling helpers into ice-covered statues. "Gotham City's mine now," Freeze roared, though there was no one there to hear him. "What could be cooler than that?"

Now, nearly six months later, Freeze was overlord of one of the city's largest areas. Only the Joker in the north and Two-Face around City Hall ruled as much territory as he did. Dozens of hoodlums had hastened to work for him, and hundreds of ordinary citizens had put themselves under his protection. And in return for a share of what little food they had, Freeze made sure no one preyed on them.

"We've set ourselves a hard target." Jim Gordon snapped shut the binoculars case, and handed it back to Batman. "Mr. Freeze is no pushover."

Standing beside him, Batman nodded. "All the

more important that we succeed," he pointed out. "If the smaller gangs see us take down Freeze, they won't dare move against us."

"Everybody ready?" Gordon whispered. Behind him, voices murmured their assent. "Then let's do it!"

"Last one to the top buys the ice creams," Robin grinned, as he and Batgirl raced off together.

The plan worked like a dream. While Gordon's Blue Boys launched a diversionary attack on the palace's eastern walls, Robin and Batgirl took care of the guards stationed in the west.

Side by side, Batman and Nightwing scaled the walls of ice with their grapnels. Halfway up, Nightwing's powerful legs pushed hard against the wall, and he swung out on the end of his line. His feet stuck straight in front of him as the line carried him inward again. Judging his moment, he let go and crashed through the window.

Batman hadn't paused in his own climb. Nightwing's job would be to neutralize Freeze's right-hand men and cut off any escape route the villain might have. It was Batman's task to face Freeze himself, in the lair Freeze had built at the castle's peak.

Far below, Batman could hear the sound of fighting as the police confronted the palace goons. By now, Robin and Batgirl ought to be working their way around the perimeter, ready to surprise the hoodlums from behind.

Barely grunting with the effort, Batman swung himself over the slippery ledge of the highest battlement. He caught a blur of movement out of the corner of his eye, and only his instincts saved him as he dived headlong across the ice. A burst of pure cryogenic energy blasted into the wall where he'd stood an instant before, gouging a massive hole in it.

Freeze stood there, resplendent in his cryo-suit, his trademark ice-gun in his hand. "Somehow, I knew it would be you," he said thinly, his finger tightening on the trigger once more. Batman was already moving away, the wrinkled soles of his boots giving his feet purchase on the slippery surface, as the cryo-burst shattered against the icy ground.

Before Freeze could aim and fire again, a swarm of tiny Batarangs arced out from Batman's hand. The villain roared in pain as they ripped into his gauntlet, their razor-sharp tips slicing through the fabric into the flesh beneath, making him drop his ice-gun.

But Freeze was far from finished. His other hand grasped the stem of a long, thick icicle hanging from the wall, and snapped it off. Swinging it like a sword, he charged at Batman.

The Dark Knight ducked agilely under the sharp icicle—but in doing so he lost his balance, his feet skidding from under him on the sheer ice. He landed hard on his back, the breath driven from his lungs by the impact.

"Relax, Batman." Freeze grinned as he raised the giant icicle in both hands, about to bring its gleaming tip plunging down into his hated foe. "Let me help you chill out—forever!"

At the very last second, Batman flung himself aside, and the icicle slammed into the ground, shattering into hundreds of pieces. As Batman rolled to his feet, his hand reached down to the sheath concealed in his boot and drew out his knife.

Frustrated, Freeze stooped to snatch up his fallen ice-gun. But Batman was faster; his knife whistled through the air, slashing deep into the plastic tube that carried cryogenic fluids through Freeze's suit. Coolant spurted out with a loud hiss.

Desperately, Freeze clutched at the torn tubing with both hands, trying to stem the flow.

Batman's flying dropkick was timed with exquisite precision. Freeze looked up, and as if in slow motion, he saw Batman sailing toward him, feetfirst. He didn't have time to duck before Batman slammed into his chest, driving him back against his own ice wall with a force that stunned him.

By the time Gordon and the others made it to the top, Freeze was tightly trussed up in a bat-line, and a new flag fluttered from the flagpole. Tomorrow, when the sun rose and people looked up, they would see the bat-symbol proudly flying above them.

"There's something wrong, Joker!"

"Let me guess, Harley. Freeze's ice palace has melted, right?"

"Worse than that," Harley Quinn groaned, and passed the binoculars to her boss. They stood together on a tree-lined road near the top of Finger Heights, the highest land in north Gotham. They and their ever-growing gang had moved into a street full of luxury houses, but already food was running short, and they had to take new turf.

Joker giggled to himself as he zoomed in on the bat-symbol flag billowing in the morning sun. "I wondered why we hadn't heard from the Bat. Well, let him enjoy his moment of triumph. It'll end soon enough—when we wrap him in his own stupid flag and bury him!"

"Like a true hero," Harley said with a smile.

Joker quickly corrected her: "Like a *dead* hero!"

There was a loud buzzing noise, and they looked up to see a sleek helicopter speeding through the air above them.

"Who could that be?" Harley wondered.

"Who cares?" Joker shrugged, his short attention span already distracted by a flock of seagulls disturbed by the chopper's passage. "If I'm not mistaken, dinner's on the wing!"

From Oracle's Log: No Man's Land, Day 175.

At last, I dare hope the tide has turned! It's been a week since the Bat-squad and my dad's men defeated Mr. Freeze. In that time, they've gone up against several other renegade villains. Nightwing and Robin faced off against Clayface, whose radioactive body could have killed them with the slightest touch.

Hardback Bock and Montoya acted as decoys to bring the villainess, Poison

Ivy, out of the jungle she'd turned Robinson Park into. Avoiding her toxic, flesh-eating plants, Batman brought her down with a Bat-bola and trapped her in a net.

And Dad finally caught up with Penguin. Like a magpie, the cackling criminal had a fatal attraction for anything that glittered. Jewelry had no value in No Man's Land—after all, you couldn't eat it or burn it—but Dad guessed Penguin's greed would get the better of him.

So when Penguin led his men on a looting expedition to the Diamond District, they found the Blue Boys waiting. Dad had staked out an upper floor, and when Penguin's thugs entered, several large nets were dropped on them from above. The whole gang was captured without a single shot being fired.

I'd just *love* to have seen the grin on Dad's face when he finally snapped the handcuffs around Penguin's wrists.

On the debit side, Dad had a blazing argument with Pettit yesterday. Seems the ex—S.W.A.T. commander had been mistreating some of the prisoners. When Dad confronted him, Pettit just cursed,

turned his back, and walked away. I hear
that he's looking to forge an alliance
with the Huntress. I don't like either
of them, but at least they'll be fighting on our side!

Several of my informants have reported sightings of a helicopter above
the city. So far, there are no clues to
whose it might be—or why it's here.

"Somehow, we have to get into the security
vaults under City Hall!"

Batman's voice was low and urgent. The members of his team furrowed their brows as, by the
light of an oil lamp, they studied the large-scale
map of the City Hall district that was pinned to the
wall.

The room had originally been a storage depot
for one of Gotham's dozens of subway stations. But
with the help of Alfred, Batman had turned it into
one of the many Batcaves that he'd established
throughout the city.

"You told us Two-Face beat you before—"
Nightwing began.

"But with Batgirl, there are four of us now,"
Robin pointed out. "And Commissioner Gordon's
men will back us up."

"Not enough," Nightwing said thoughtfully. "According to Oracle, Killer Croc has now joined forces with Two-Face. City Hall must be the best-defended position in town."

"It is," Batman conceded. "But it's imperative that we get into those vaults. Every record of every citizen is held there—births, deaths, marriages. And most important, the title deeds to every property in the city! Without them, we've no chance of ever setting things to rights again."

They spent the next hour devising strategies and plans. But at the end of it, they seemed no closer to finding the solution.

The helicopter circled lazily, as if to give its occupants an overview of the city, before coming down to land on the helipad at the Gotham Knights Stadium. Normally, Air Force jets would have chased the intruder off. But once they'd established voice contact with the chopper—once they found out who was inside it—the jets turned and streaked away.

One of the stadium walls had collapsed completely during the quake. Inside, the once-pristine field on which a thousand baseball games had been played was fast turning into a massive weed-patch.

As the rotor blades slowed and stopped, a door in the chopper's side slid open and a tall, handsome figure with long, flowing hair stepped out. Dressed in an expensive silk designer suit, he looked like a European aristrocrat or some fabulously wealthy pop star.

"Ah! It's good to be home," Nicholas Scratch said with feeling, although he'd never been to Gotham before in his life.

Behind him, six of the most grotesque beings ever to set foot outside a freak show spilled from the chopper door. Their skin was dry and leathery, their eyes glittering red. They had been men once— before Scratch had practiced his gene-manipulating skills on them, turning them into misshapen monsters totally obedient to him alone. For unknown to any of his thousands of admirers, Scratch had a dark secret that he kept well hidden.

Nicholas Scratch had spent all his adult life as an astronomer. And a loser. Everything he did went wrong; every money-making scheme backfired. It seemed as if the dreams of fame and fortune that haunted him would never be fulfilled. Then one night, as he was scanning the cosmos with his telescope, something incredible happened. A beam of bright blue light appeared from out of nowhere, shining directly down the barrel of the telescope into Scratch's eyes.

The shock knocked him unconscious. When he awoke hours later, he was no longer the loser he'd always been. An unknown cosmic energy surged through his body, giving him unbelievable strength and awareness. His mind raced continually, sifting, selecting, scheming. And perhaps best of all, he found he had an almost hypnotic ability to influence other men to do exactly what he wanted them to.

His newfound powers quickly brought him fame and wealth. But they weren't enough. Scratch wanted more: He wanted a whole city to call his own. And when the quake struck Gotham, he saw his chance—and seized it.

Now, he was about to reap what he had sown.

Hurrying to keep up, the men followed their boss as he climbed easily up the rubble of the broken stadium wall. By the time they reached him he was standing at the very top, gazing out over the ruins.

"Gotham—a suitable case for rebuilding," Scratch said cheerfully.

"But, Mr. Scratch," one of his men said, puzzled, "it was your influence on Congress that led to the city being abandoned!"

"All part of the Scratch master plan, my mindless minion," his boss replied. "I shall admit to Congress that I made a mistake—the city should be saved. They won't be able to resist me. And who better to be on the end of all those billion-dollar federal rebuilding grants than me?"

"I don't understand." The same man spoke again. "Why would the government give you money when you don't even own a single building here?"

"Dolt!" Scratch's cheerful façade slipped for a moment, revealing the true nature of the man beneath. His hand lashed out to slap his creation hard around the face, jerking its head back. "How could you ever expect to understand the greatest mind on Earth?"

Before the quake, Gotham real estate was valued at hundreds of billions of dollars. Afterward, it was worth only a fraction of that. And once Scratch had used his hypnotic powers to sway Congress, denying the stricken city federal aid, its value sank to zero.

Now all Scratch had to do was get his hands on the computerized records in the vaults at City Hall. Back at his headquarters, his brilliant mind would have no trouble hacking into the disks and changing titles so they showed that he, Scratch, had bought almost all of Gotham before the quake. Hundreds of thousands had died—there would be no argument from them. The survivors were dispersed all over America; by the time they even suspected foul play, Scratch's lawyers would have everything sewn up. He would not only own the entire city, but the federal government would give him the money to rebuild it. Genius!

"Here, you ugly brutes," Scratch snapped, and like pets with their master, the men clustered around him. "Your first priority is to steal the records from City Hall."

"The gangs are sure to try to stop us," one of the men commented.

"And Batman!" another put in.

"Oh, well." Scratch smiled warmly, as if he was about to suggest inviting Batman over for dinner. "You'll just have to kill them all!"

CHAPTER 9

THE MAIN ATTRACTION

From Oracle's Log: No Man's Land, Day 201.

The city is split almost equally in three parts: Joker has all of the north, Two-Face and Killer Croc lord over most of the south and east, while Dad and Batman hold the west and center.

Batman has had everyone on permanent alert since we heard that Nicholas Scratch had been in Gotham. News from the outside world says that Scratch is trying to persuade Congress to go back on its decision to abandon the city. Why, we don't know, although Batman seems to have his suspicions.

He and Nightwing have been working on one of the four-wheel-drive Batmobiles, turning it into some kind of

war machine. Our spies tell us Two-Face
has stationed machine guns at each corner of the City Hall roof. But when anyone asks Batman when we're going to make
our move, he just cautions patience and
says our chance will come.

Batman was right, their chance did come.

Robin and Batgirl were out on a surveillance
mission, using night-lenses to try to determine just
how many gunmen Two-Face had on his payroll.
What they saw surprised them—and galvanized
Batman into action.

"Oracle?" Robin's voice crackled through the
walkie-talkie. "Tell Batman there are six figures, all
armed, making their way toward City Hall. We can't
get a definite ID on them, but they sure look weird!"

Immediately, Oracle relayed the message to Batman. He was silent for a minute, as if contemplating
all the possibilities. Then he made his decision.

"It seems someone else is about to raid Two-
Face. Pass it on, Oracle: I want everybody ready to
go in ten minutes. And see if you can contact Pettit
and Huntress—we could use all the help we can get
on this one!"

* * *

The heavily modified Batmobile moved slowly along the street, its powerful engines struggling with the extra weight it carried. Batman and Nightwing had welded dozens of solid steel plates into a protective framework around it, so it looked more like a moving bank vault than a car. Protected by the solid steel, Gordon's Blue Boys marched alongside the Batmobile, looking for all the world like some medieval army about to ransack the enemy's castle.

Suddenly, a yell followed by a barrage of gunshots sounded from the rear of City Hall. Scratch's creatures had launched their own attack.

Batman slipped his steel-clad vehicle into a lower gear, and steered it straight for the broad granite steps that swept up to the huge front door.

A deadly hail of bullets rained down from the machine guns Two-Face had stationed on the roof, but the Batmobile's steel cladding did its job well. Marching beneath the protective canopy, Jim Gordon and his forces would never forget the noise those bullets made as they ricocheted above their heads.

Then, acting in unison, Nightwing, Robin, and Batgirl launched their own precision assaults from the rooftops. They lobbed phosphor flares from the upper floors of adjacent buildings to land close to the machine-gun nests, temporarily blinding the gunners and allowing the trio to attack at will.

Robin leapt on them with his bo staff swinging in his hands, its weighted end spelling instant unconsciousness to every thug it struck. Nightwing and Batgirl, meanwhile, relied on their fists and feet.

Within minutes, the guns had fallen silent, as the tanklike Batmobile rumbled up the stairs below.

Gunning the engine for maximum power, Batman steered straight at the heavy entrance door. There was a loud splintering of wood, and then they were in.

"You all know your assignments," Batman called out as he slid from the driver's cab. A Batarang streaked from his hand, to thud heavily into the head of a hoodlum rushing at him with a baseball bat. "Let's do what we came for!"

The Blue Boys' objective was simple: secure the entire ground floor, then start to work their way upward, while Nightwing and the other two crime fighters made their way down from the roof. They were to meet in the middle, on the fourth floor.

Everyone had been issued knockout gas pellets,

in case they ran into Killer Croc. Although not invulnerable, Croc's tough, scaly hide was impervious to all but the most carefully aimed bullet; gas was the surest way to take the monster out.

Meanwhile, Batman fought his way down to the basement vaults. Two-Face had well over a hundred men at arms, but less than a third actually had guns. The rest were wielding nail-studded baseball bats, improvised spears, crossbows, and a range of home-made weapons.

There were three thugs with bows and arrows waiting at the top of the basement stairs. Without even slowing in his rush, Batman dug into a pouch in his Utility Belt and pulled out a handful of steel ball bearings. He rolled them along the floor at their feet, and by the time he reached the men they were skidding and swaying around, desperately trying to maintain their balance.

In a flurry of blows and karate kicks, Batman felled them all.

But this was only a skirmish; the real battle was yet to come.

Jim Gordon edged along the wall of the grand Council Chamber. A dozen candles stood on the massive oak conference table in the center of the room, but their flames brought feeble light to only part of it.

Gordon had left his men fighting their way along the wide corridor outside, figuring he could flank the opposition if there was an exit at the room's far end.

"Good to see you again . . . partner." The voice issued from a recess halfway down the chamber, and the last word was said with such contempt that Gordon knew it could be only one man: Two-Face.

Smoothly, Gordon dropped to one knee, turned, and squeezed off a shot from his gun. It thudded harmlessly into the paneled woodwork.

Before he could figure out where his foe had gone, Gordon felt the sudden pressure of a gun barrel against the back of his head.

"We had a deal, you and I," Two-Face hissed. "I helped you out when you asked me. But do you help me in return? No, you do not."

The villain knocked the gun from Gordon's hand before he went on: "Instead, you attack my territory. You shoot at my men. The acts of a traitor, Commissioner. And we all know what happens to traitors. They're *executed.*"

The policeman's mind was racing, turning over every possibility of escape. But he had no gun, and his back was to Two-Face. He'd take a bullet before he could move even a few inches. Beads of cold sweat broke out on his forehead as the maniac cocked the trigger.

Nicholas Scratch loped down the fire-escape stairs, his three surviving men close behind him. The other three lay dead, mowed down by Two-Face's hirelings; but they'd served their master well before they died, and the bodies of a dozen gangsters were sprawled around them.

Scratch had created these monsters especially for this job, knowing he'd have to overwhelm some of Gotham's toughest criminals in order to achieve his objective. No one in the outside world was aware of their existence, and Scratch reasoned that in the bedlam and confusion of No Man's Land, the redesigned men would never be connected to him.

He had heard the gunfire and commotion issuing from all over City Hall, and guessed it meant someone else was in the process of an assault. *Excellent! That will make my task that much easier!*

The heavy fire door at the foot of the stairs was

locked and barred, but Scratch had the strength of ten men. A couple of hefty kicks, and the door crashed open.

"You stay here," Scratch told his men. "Make sure no one follows me."

As he ran down the stairs to the basement, Scratch was already mentally composing the victorious speech he'd make to Congress about the rebuilding of Gotham—a city that the records would show he owned almost in its entirety.

The vault room was huge, covering an area the size of a football field underneath City Hall and its plaza. Banks of gray-green filing cabinets stood in rows, their drawers open, the documents they'd once contained long since looted by hoodlums as fuel for their fires.

Batman ignored the cabinets, heading straight for the large walk-in safe; a notice on its circular door read COMPUTER FILES. That door had remained solidly locked since the day of the quake.

Deftly, Batman extracted a small package of plastic explosive from his Utility Belt and wedged it against the lock. He flicked on the mini-timer, then retreated behind a filing cabinet.

Less than a minute later, there was a muffled bang. Seconds after that, Batman was inside the vault, ignoring the acrid smoke from the explosion as he used a flashlight to browse among the racks of computer disks. Births, deaths, marriages were in the first section. Quickly, he moved on, his hand closing around three small disks.

Suddenly, as if alerted by some sixth sense, he ducked his head. Just in time. Killer Croc's massive balled fist whistled past him, slamming hard into the wall of the vault.

"Welcome to City Hall, little man," Croc hissed menacingly between his sharp fangs. "Welcome to your death!"

"Wait!" Jim Gordon cried out. "You can't shoot me, it would be going against your own code! You have to let your coin decide!"

"Ah, yes. My coin." Two-Face's grotesque features contorted into what passed for a grin. "You're right, of course. My coin always decides for me."

The villain felt in the pocket of his two-tone jacket and brought out his silver dollar, resting it on the curled forefinger of his left hand. "If it lands scarred side up, I shoot you," he said lightly. "Unscarred side, I slit your throat with a knife!"

His thumb flicked up and struck the edge of the coin, flipping it high into the air.

Gordon darted a glance back over his shoulder and saw that Two-Face was distractedly gazing up at the coin as it tumbled end over end. It was now or never!

The Commissioner straightened his legs and shot up from the floor. His shoulder caught Two-Face under the arm, wrenching it upward, causing him to drop his gun in surprise. The coin and the gun hit the floor together, but Gordon didn't even hear them. He was twisting from the waist, throwing every ounce of power into the straight right jab that took Two-Face perfectly on the chin.

The villain didn't even gasp as his eyes closed, his legs buckled, and his body collapsed to the floor.

Killer Croc's lizardlike eyes glittered coldly as he lunged with both hands at Batman. Before he became a villain, Croc had been a championship wrestler, one of the best in the world. He even gave demonstrations, wrestling eighteen-foot alligators brought especially from the Florida swamps. Batman knew it would be a serious mistake to allow Croc to get too close.

The Dark Knight jumped lithely to one side. Bracing himself against the steel wall, he brought both feet up off the floor and kicked out with all his strength. His boots caught Croc in the stomach, winding him, sending the villain reeling back out of the vault and slamming into a filing cabinet that fell over under the impact.

Croc gave a muffled grunt as he righted himself, his huge hand closing around a long file drawer that had slid out when the cabinet fell. Batman was diving through the air toward him, intending to press home his advantage, when Croc swung the heavy drawer like a club.

The blow struck Batman with a stunning impact. Groaning, he fell to the floor, clutching at his right shoulder and upper arm; they were rapidly going numb. Before he could recover, Croc dived. Batman exhaled sharply as the villain's crushing weight landed on him. Then Croc's hands were around his neck, squeezing with unbelievable force.

Batman knew he would be unconscious within seconds.

Desperately, he maneuvered his body so that his

left arm was free. He fumbled at his Utility Belt, knowing that if he failed now, he would never get another chance.

Croc's grip tightened even more, and red lights started to flash in Batman's eyes as darkness swirled about him. His finger flipped the cap off a tiny percussion grenade, and he tossed it upward to arc over Croc's shoulder. All of the grenade's energy was released in one almighty *BANG!* that seemed to echo around the whole basement.

Croc yelled hoarsely, releasing his grip to paw at his ears as he stumbled to his feet.

Batman's cowl spared him the worst of the noise, but he still felt as if his senses had been scrambled. He knew he had to follow through quickly.

Croc was staggering away in pain as a triple-weighted Bat-bola spun through the air and wrapped itself around his ankles. The floor shook as he fell.

A gas pellet shattered suddenly by Croc's head, then another, and a third. Thick, cloying fumes enveloped him as he tried to lurch to his feet. He coughed hard, and his reptilian eyes began to lose all focus.

Fighting against the pain that raged down the

right side of his body, Batman stooped to grab the moaning villain by the ankles. Exerting all his strength, he dragged Croc across the floor and back into the vault. Swiftly, he slammed the thick steel door, trapping the villain inside. Even Killer Croc wouldn't be able to smash his way out of that.

Grimacing with the effort, Batman leaned against a cabinet to regain his breath. No bones seemed to be broken, but he was going to have some serious bruises.

"Looks like someone's done my work for me."

Batman recognized the voice at once. It was the voice of the man who had argued for Gotham's demise. Slowly, Batman looked up.

Nicholas Scratch stood there, gun in hand.

"What are you doing here, Scratch?" Batman snarled.

"Why, I've come to stake my claim on Gotham City. Once Congress falls into line, and they decide to give federal aid, Gotham will be worth billions of dollars. Hundreds of billions. And it'll all be mine—" Scratch jerked his gun up so it pointed directly at Batman's head. "Just as soon as I take possession of the ownership records, it all belongs to me. Hand them over!"

"I don't know what you're talking about," Batman bluffed.

Scratch's finger started to tighten on the trigger. "Suit yourself," he shrugged. "I'll shoot you and then take the records!"

"All right," Batman said grudgingly. "You win!" His hand went to a pocket in his cape and pulled out three computer disks. "They're yours." He tossed them to the floor directly in front of Scratch. "Gotham City's yours."

Scratch's eyes never left Batman's as he stooped to pick up the disks.

"I really ought to kill you now." Scratch grinned triumphantly. "But I think I'll wait. When Gotham is registered in my name, I'll have you arrested and booted out!" Disks in hand, he started to back away. "You'll be the laughingstock of the city."

Batman stood motionless, his eyes grim. Only when Scratch had reached the stairs did Batman allow himself a small smile.

Nicholas Scratch was in for a nasty shock.

CHAPTER 10

METHOD IN MADNESS

From Oracle's Log: No Man's Land, Day 219.

As the summer heat climbs, so does the tension in the air. Two-Face and Killer Croc may be beaten, but now Joker has arrived on the scene, his army of more than a thousand swarming through the streets. Only about a tenth of them are criminals, though—the others have all been press-ganged by the Joker and forced to fight for him on pain of death.

The ironic thing is, I heard on my satellite com-link that Nicholas Scratch's appeal to Congress has been successful. Seems the President is already working on a bill to rescind No Man's Land.

I just hope it hasn't come too late!

* * *

The sun was sinking low in a bloodred sky when the sounds of people singing drifted across Kochman Square. *"Oh, when the saints go marching in . . ."*

In his makeshift office in the Police HQ building, Jim Gordon's ears pricked up and his mouth curved in a small smile. He hadn't heard singing since before Black Monday. The voices were out of tune, and the rhythm was way out of synch, but to Gordon's ears it sounded great.

"Oh, I want to be in that number . . ." Humming to himself, Gordon crossed to his window and looked out. What he saw there wiped the smile from his lips and made his blood run cold.

About a hundred people—men, women, and children—were marching five abreast up the slope of a ruined avenue toward the far end of the square, singing at the top of their voices. They were roped together in an improvised harness, dragging a huge oil delivery tanker behind them. On the tanker's side, the name of the company that owned it had been painted out, to be replaced with large, gaudy letters that read: THE JOKEMOBILE. Behind it was a vast throng, and even from here Gordon could see that many of them were armed.

The Commissioner turned as a figure appeared by his side. It was Foley, for the most part recovered from the beating he'd taken at the hands of Killer Croc.

"What the heck's going on, Commish? Some kind of street party?"

"Hardly," Gordon said thinly. He wiped beads of perspiration from his forehead—and they weren't just caused by the heat. "Better warn Batman and the others. He's here. The Joker!"

Down on the street, the cops on guard watched, bemused, as the strange procession came to a halt at the opposite side of the square, under the shadows of a ruined shopping mall. People came hurrying from their living quarters to see what was going on, and by the time Jim Gordon had made it downstairs and outside, several hundred spectators had gathered.

Suddenly, an access hatch on top of the tanker was thrown open, and the singing voices died away as two figures clambered out.

"Roll up, roll up," Harley Quinn chanted into the megaphone she held in one hand, "for all the fun of the fair!" The madwoman grinned as her amplified words reverberated around the square. "We have jugglers! We have clowns! We have death-defying trapeze artistes!"

Standing beside her atop the tanker, Joker scowled. "Hey, I'm the main attraction here," he snapped. He snatched the megaphone from her and raised it to his lips.

"People of Gotham," the Clown Prince of Crime began, "I offer you this puzzle: What's the difference between one hundred singing citizens and one hundred corpses?"

Joker paused and waited, but the silence was broken only by the fading echoes of his voice. "Give up?" he yelled. Patience was never the Joker's strong point. "Well, here's the punch line—" He fumbled in his pocket, and held up a small electronic transmitter. "A radio-controlled bomb! Hahaha!"

Jim Gordon looked around him. No sign of Batman or Nightwing or any of the others. His hand closed around the revolver in its holster under his jacket, but he found no reassurance there. The assault on Two-Face and Croc had all but exhausted the Blue Boys' stocks of ammunition, and Gordon's gun—like those of so many of his men—was empty.

Summoning up all his courage, Gordon took a deep breath and strode forward.

"I'm in charge here, Joker," he called out. "If you have anything to say, you say it to me!"

"Ah, my old friend, Commissioner Gordon!" Joker's eyes glinted malevolently. "Tell me, sir— how's your lovely daughter?"

Gordon felt dark emotions well up inside him. Ever since the Joker had shot Barbara, condemning her to life in a wheelchair, Gordon had harbored a burning hatred for the madman. But hatred would do him—and Gotham—no good now. Biting back his bile, the Commissioner fought to keep his voice steady: "I'm ordering you to surrender, and your men to lay down their weapons. You're all under arrest!"

"Hahahahahahaha!" Joker clutched his sides, laughing fit to burst. It was a full minute before he recovered enough to continue speaking: "You've got it all wrong, Gordon old boy. *I'm* the one issuing the ultimatum!" He gestured toward the people harnessed to the tanker with the radio transmitter. "Every one of these innocent citizens has a small quantity of high explosive taped to their bodies. When I press this button, they all go *KA-BOOM!*

Hahaha!" His laughter broke off abruptly, and there was a deadly chill in his voice as he added: "You have five minutes, Gordon. Unless you surrender to me by then . . . it's bye-bye citizens!"

Gordon's heart sank. Without ammunition, he could see no way out of this impasse.

Joker again raised the megaphone to his bright red lips. "Oh, and one more thing, Commish, old buddy, old pal," the maniac ordered. "You have to hand over the Batman to me. Personally." His voice sank a full octave lower. "I'm afraid I have some *very* bad things in store for him!"

Once more Joker's insane, unnerving laughter echoed throughout the square, and beside him Harley Quinn capered around like some medieval court jester. "Five minutes, Gordon. And the count-down starts—now!"

His mind numb, his feet like lead weights, Gordon trudged back to the sidewalk outside Police HQ. Foley hurried to join him.

"There's no sign of Batman, sir—or the others," the officer told him. "You don't think . . . I mean, he wouldn't abandon us again, would he?"

Jim Gordon shook his head adamantly. "He didn't abandon us the first time, Foley," he said quietly. "It was all a misunderstanding. Wherever Batman is, whatever he's doing, I have full confidence in him."

Fifty feet above the square, watching the scene below from a shattered window, Batman crouched in the ruined shopping mall.

"Four minutes, Commissioner!" he heard the Joker shout.

Batman held his walkie-talkie close to his mask as he whispered: "Everybody in position? Over."

There was a short burst of static; then Robin's voice crackled: "Batgirl and I are ready." After a few seconds' delay, Nightwing replied: "Almost there, boss. I need another minute."

Batman nodded to himself. He only hoped they had another minute; almost directly below him he could see Joker toying with the transmitter that would detonate the bombs.

"Careful, Joker!" Harley Quinn's words drifted up, and Batman leaned out slightly to get a better view.

On the tanker roof, Joker was stroking the transmitter as if it was a pet cat, his thumb hovering over the red detonator button. "Oh, let's just blow them now," he was saying. "That really would be fun!"

"But then we won't have any hostages to threaten, and Gordon's men will attack us, and all these people will be killed!"

"I know, Harley." Joker's eyes met hers. "What a joke that would be, don't you think?"

They both began to giggle uncontrollably, and Harley's hand reached out toward the box. "Okay," she agreed, "but let me press the button."

"Say please."

"Please, Joker."

"Pretty please?"

High above, Batman snapped into his radio: "No more time, Nightwing. It's now or never!"

Then he was on his feet, a bat-line snaking from his hand. Its grapnel caught on a ledge of the building opposite, and Batman launched himself into the air.

On top of the tanker, Harley fluttered her eyelashes at her lunatic boss. "Pretty please," she simpered, her finger creeping toward the detonator.

Suddenly, a shadow fell across them and they both looked up in surprise—Batman dropped toward them like some grim avenging angel.

"Whoops! It's the spoilsport himself," Joker began. His thumb sought the detonator button—but it was too late. Batman's feet slammed into him, knocking the transmitter from his hand. The force of the impact knocked Joker back, tripping over the edge of the hatch. The megaphone went flying from his grip as, arms flailing desperately to restore his balance, the maniac fell through the hatch into the belly of the tanker.

Without pausing, Batman dropped through after him, his hand grabbing the metal hatch and pulling it closed behind him with a loud clang.

Momentarily bewildered, Harley Quinn tried to figure out what to do. But even as she stooped to try to wrest open the hatch, Batgirl swung down to land beside her. They exchanged a flurry of blows, but Harley was no match for a girl who'd been trained by the world's top assassin. The fight was over in seconds, and Harley lay senseless on the tanker roof.

On the ground, Robin raced out from his hiding place behind a stack of rubble. He leapfrogged over a couple of the Joker's minions who were intent on retrieving the fallen detonator box and whisked it away from them.

Close to the harnessed hostages, a storm drain was suddenly thrown open. Nightwing emerged from it, and began slicing at the captives' ropes with a long, sharp blade.

Without their insane leaders to direct them, the Joker's armed thugs didn't know what to do. Several of them raised their guns, threatening to open fire on the innocent spectators. But the majority of the Joker's army was made up of people who'd been forced to take his side; realizing that this was their chance, they turned on their captors and swamped them in a seething mass of humanity.

"You know what your trouble is?"

Inside the tanker was nothing but two deck chairs. Joker's voice was high and strident, but it boomed metallically in the confined space as he and Batman faced each other.

"You have no sense of fun!"

As he said the last word, Joker's fist shot out and caught Batman full in the face. He jerked his head back, tasting blood; he'd forgotten how fast the Joker could be. As the maniac swung again, Batman grabbed his fist in an iron grip.

"Killing isn't fun," the Dark Knight hissed between clenched teeth. His other hand chopped down, held rigid in a karate strike that took Joker on the shoulder and numbed all the muscles of his left arm.

"Hurting innocent people isn't fun either," Batman went on, the same rigid fingers now digging into Joker's belly. The maniac gasped and bent double. As Batman released his grip, Joker fell back over a deck chair and crashed to the tanker floor.

"The day you realize that," Batman finished, "is the day you can rejoin the human race!"

"Human race!" Joker sneered. "I run in my own race. That way, I always win!" From the floor, his right foot shot out in a scything kick that caught Batman behind the knee. As Batman stumbled back against the tanker wall, Joker sprang to his feet and his hand clamped over the bulb that led to the plastic flower he always wore in his lapel.

"You're boring, boring, boring!" he cackled, pressing hard on the bulb.

Batman saw the thin jet of acid spurt from the flower's center, and threw himself into a perfect backflip that carried him to the tanker's opposite end. The potent acid struck the tanker wall, and there was a loud hiss as it ate into the metal.

"Not fond of acid?" Joker grinned evilly, and depressed a stud on the fish-shaped ring he wore on his index finger. An inch-long spike sprang out from one of the fish's eye sockets, and its sharp point glistened with an oily liquid. "Then how about poison?"

Joker lashed out with a backhand blow. Batman dodged aside, and the poisoned spike missed his face by less than an inch. He didn't wait for Joker to strike again, but brought his foot up in a high karate kick that crushed Joker's hand against the tanker wall and broke the spike off.

Joker shrieked with pain, then shrieked again as Batman drove straight into his ribs.

"It's over," Batman said softly, and his piledriving fist exploded in the villain's face.

Joker's eyes began to glaze over. "Yes, it's over," he agreed, his voice barely audible. He fell back against the tanker wall, and slid slowly to the floor. Batman had to strain to hear his final words before he lapsed into unconsciousness: "But it was fun while it lasted."

Then the hatch was opened from outside, and

Batman looked up to see the faces of his team framed in the circular opening. Robin gave him a thumbs-up signal, and grinned.

"Nice work, boss!"

In all the excitement, no one had heard the sound of the helicopter overhead. No one had noticed it landing a few blocks away. But now an angry Nicholas Scratch shoved his way through the throng toward Batman, as he leapt down from the tanker.

"You tricked me!" Scratch pointed accusingly at Batman, his face red with fury.

Batman shrugged. "Is that so?"

"You know darn well it is," Scratch raged. "Congress heeded my pleas. They've decided to open Gotham up again. But when I logged on to those computer disks, to change legal ownership of the city to me, what did I find?"

"Let me guess," Nightwing said innocently, standing by Batman's side. "You expected to have the property ownership details. But instead, you found that you had lists of every birth, death, and marriage in Gotham since records began, right?"

"Batman gave me the wrong disks! He must have switched them in the vaults!" Scratch fumed. "He cheated me!"

Jim Gordon stepped forward, not caring to disguise the look of contempt in his eyes as he glared at Scratch. "I have the original disks," Gordon said, "showing the *true* owners of Gotham. And your name appears nowhere on them, Scratch."

Gordon shoved his face threateningly close to Scratch's before he continued: "I'm the law here once again. And I say, unless you leave at once, you're going to find yourself locked up on Blackgate Island with all the other crooks and hoodlums!"

"On what charge?"

"Conspiracy to steal city property." Gordon smiled, but it was the smile of a tiger sizing up its prey. "And once I start to investigate your past, who knows what else I might turn up?"

Scratch was almost speechless. It was obvious that Gordon meant every word he said—and Nicholas Scratch had far too many secrets for him to risk a police probe into his private affairs. Cursing at Gordon, he spun away on his heel.

"I'll get you for this, Batman!" he vowed as he

stormed off. "Someday, someplace, I'll make you pay for humiliating me!"

"I look forward to it," Batman said simply.

From Oracle's Log: No Man's Land, Day 240.

In the end, it turned out Scratch had done us all a favor. Whatever strings he had pulled in Congress, whatever influence he had used on the country's leading politicians, it had worked. Unfortunately for Scratch, without the ownership records to forge, he personally gained no benefit from his evil scheme.

The Army pulled down the barriers today. They've already started building temporary bridges, and they're airdropping food and supplies. The construction companies will arrive soon, backed by Bruce Wayne and federal aid. The people will follow them. One day, in a year, or maybe two, Gotham City will be alive again.

Sometimes, late at night, I sit by my window and watch, hoping to catch a glimpse of Batman or Robin soaring over the city roofs. Or even the new Batgirl.

I still feel a pang of regret, seeing someone else in the costume that used to be mine. But Cassandra and I have become close friends, and I couldn't resent her, even if I wanted to.

Now that it's all over, there's no need for me to continue keeping this record. I can return to my anonymous life as Oracle, doing what I do, helping this city in any way I can.

Maybe some day, years in the future, someone will listen to these tapes—and learn the true story of what went on in the hell that was once No Man's Land.

EPILOGUE

Moonlight flitted across the cemetery, tinting the cold, white marble with pale gold.

Batman stood by his parents' grave, his head bowed, savoring the peace and quiet. Only blocks away, the construction companies were at work on twenty-four-hour shifts. Their generators hummed, and spotlamps lit up the night, bringing light to streets that for many months had known only darkness.

But here there was just the sighing of the light wind, and the first leaves of autumn rustling on the trees.

"So much has happened in the past year," Batman said, half-aloud, as if his parents could hear him. "I've learned that no man is an island. We all need help sometimes. Even heroes."

He paused, deep in thought.

Civilization is people working together. It can't be forced on anyone. A city without civilization is a city without life. Like Gotham itself, Batman had faced his darkest hour . . . and both of them had come safely through to the other side.

He took a single long-stemmed rose from the folds of his cape and laid it carefully on the grave. Its deep red petals seemed to glow in the moonlight.

"I kept my promise," he said quietly. "The city lives again."

Then he was gone, swallowed by the darkness, swinging away into the rooftops. And for the first time since Black Monday, his heart was singing.

About the Author

ALAN GRANT was born in Bristol, England, in 1949. His grandmother taught him to read at the age of three, using *Batman* and other adventure comics as her textbooks, and he has been a comic-book fan ever since. After leaving school he edited wildlife, romance, and fashion magazines before becoming a freelance writer. He produced a successful run of teenage true-confession stories before returning to his first love: comics. With longtime writing partner John Wagner, he scripted *Judge Dredd* and a dozen other science fiction series for the British comic-book sensation *2000AD*. Since 1987, Alan has written almost two hundred different Batman stories, including the hugely popular *Batman/Spawn* and *Batman/Judge Dredd* team-ups. He is currently

working on several Batman projects, as well as Ter-
minator for Dark Horse Comics and a range of
graphic novels for the LEGO toy company. Alan
Grant lives and works in a Gothic mansion in the
Scottish border country with his wife and guardian
angel, Sue, and a strange cat named Thompson.